The Con Man's Daughter

By Teresa Trent

A Redbird Creek
Romance

Chapter 1

Anna Holman stood in the luxurious high-ceilinged lobby of the Redbird Creek Country Club. It was smaller than she remembered. The green velvet club chairs had been replaced by a set of overstuffed floral patterned barrel chairs. Near the front of the lobby was the bright white door of the manager's office and next to that a bulletin board with a schedule of meetings and activities at the club. Returning here—the place to which she once felt entitled—was humbling. Although in some ways it seemed like a lifetime ago, it hadn't been that long since she walked these halls with her friends. They spent their days worrying about crushes on boys and who was wearing what. At the time, those things took priority in her world. Not so much now. The pack of girls she ran with back in high school were the most popular in school and merciless when it came to judging others. Why not? She and her friends came from the best families, lived in the nicest houses, and never ever had to worry about money. Only poor people worried about money.

She summoned the courage she needed to get through the next hour. The old Anna would never have done that. Things were different now. Her life had changed. Drastically. She shifted and sensed unsteadiness in her right heel. The black pumps wowed her when she first bought them in New York, and the money she paid for those shoes would cover a month's rent in Redbird Creek. That was if she could find a place she could afford. No matter how much you paid for a pair of shoes, when the glue gave out, it gave out.

"You're Anna Holman. I'd recognize you anywhere." The nasally voice echoed moments in her past.

Anna turned around.

Gladys Ledbetter, known to the old Anna and her snobby friends as Goopy Gladys, raised a small hand. "Remember me?" Goopy wore gabardine pants the color of dirt and a white silk blouse that was partially tucked in.

Back in high school, Anna remembered calling Gladys an unmade bed. She and her friends had made fun of Gladys's appearance almost daily.

"Goop..." Anna stopped herself. "Gladys? It's nice to see you. I'm sorry. I didn't realize you were sitting there." Teenager Anna wouldn't have even conversed with her, lest her friends discover she'd been socializing with an undesirable.

"I walked in while you were staring at your shoes. Nice. Did you get those at Walmart?"

Quickly assessing Gladys's attire, there was no doubt in Anna's mind this woman did most, if not all, her shopping at Walmart.

"Uh, not quite."

"Are you here for the job?"

"Yes." Anna's answer was short, both because she'd never been Gladys's friend and because she was a little embarrassed. The great Anna Holman was applying for a job in front of Goopy Gladys. Would this make her think they were buddies now? Anna wasn't sure if she was ready for that. Would Gladys take the opportunity to bring Anna down another notch? She wouldn't blame her if she did—she had to admit she'd deserve it.

"Me too." Gladys gave an eager smile and nodded like the two were now official applying-for-the-same-job buddies.

And now Anna was even more embarrassed. They were not only applying for the same job, but they were discussing it. No one discussed anything with Goopy. They talked *about* her, not *to* her.

"Excuse me?"

Gladys spoke a little louder, as if Anna had a hearing impairment. "I said, me too."

"Anna? Is that you?" McKinzie Carmichael, a stunning redhead, came in wearing a white-and-blue-striped tennis sweater tied around her neck. A short white tennis skirt showcased her long, tan legs, and she wore a pair of sunglasses perched on her head. Her face had thinned out some, making her even more beautiful than Anna remembered in high school. McKinzie extended her arms wide for a welcoming hug. "How long has it been? What a wonderful surprise."

Anna sucked in a breath and as she did, the heel on her shoe snapped like a pixie stick, and Anna found herself three inches shorter on one side. "It's good to see you, McKinzie. Ten years, I guess?"

Luckily, McKinzie didn't seem to notice Anna was teetering on an invisible heel.

"This is fabulous!" McKinzie waved her hand in the air to emphasize her point. "What brings you back? This day keeps getting better and better."

Anna noticed the absence of a wedding ring, which made her question whether McKinzie was still single or a victim of the divorce wars. McKinzie might have gone through several husbands since Anna had last seen her. Anna herself never married.

McKinzie glanced over at Gladys and whispered to Anna behind her hand. "They must be short of wait staff if they're hiring Goopy. She'll probably sneeze all over the food." She gave a brief laugh, and Anna forced a smile, even though Goopy was close enough to hear everything.

"Ten years. Hard to imagine, isn't it?" Anna wobbled slightly as she struggled to level her feet. Surely McKinzie would notice the heel laying on the floor, a dead soldier in the battle of fashion.

"I know what you mean. Time flies when you're having fun, or whatever it is they say." McKinzie pulled out her phone. "Let me call Wendy. She's been so busy with her new fiancé, but surely, she'll have time to catch up with you. We *have* to do lunch today. You're free, aren't you?"

"Uh," Anna stuttered. "Not today. I have an appointment."

McKinzie slipped her phone back in her pocket and reached out and took a strand of Anna's dark blond ringlets. It was a little shorter than she wore it in high school. Her hair curled naturally, but still took work to make it behave.

"Getting your highlights done? You look like you need a little touch-up."

Anna was silent for a moment. "Yes. Way overdue. But maybe we can get together another day. You know how it is being back in town. Busy, busy, busy."

"Of course." McKinzie put her hand over her mouth as if to hold in her excitement. She overplayed it for sure, but insincere surprise was the thing to do when greeting an old friend at the country club. "Are you moving back into your old house?" Anna tried to answer but McKinzie kept talking. "Good! That couple living there is so, you know, *bookish*. Teachers or something. How are your father and mother? Are they with you—"

Before McKinzie uttered another unwanted question, Anna stopped her, finding herself rushing her words. "N-No. It's me." She pulled out her phone to check the time, even though she knew exactly what time it was. "I have to go."

McKinzie grabbed the phone out of her hand before Anna was able to put it away and tapped in something. "Let me give you my number. That way, when you're available, we can get together." She hit a button, making her own phone ring. "And there we have it. I have your number." She handed back the phone. "We have so much to catch up on, girl."

McKinzie gave Anna one more hug and proceeded in the direction of the women's locker room. Anna recognized her perfume, Poison. An older scent, but one McKinzie loved.

"Miss Holman?" A tall man in his fifties with a gray pencil-thin mustache stepped out of the manager's office. He wore a crisply pressed navy suit, white shirt, and paisley tie.

"Yes?"

"How do you do? I'm Alan Partridge, manager of the Redbird Creek Country Club. Shall we talk in my office?"

Anna picked up her bag, broken heel, and portfolio and followed Alan, limping on the one good shoe. As she bobbed across the floor, she pulled out a copy of her resume.

"Please, have a seat." He motioned to a maroon padded chair positioned next to a homey, brown-paneled wall.

Anna was grateful for the seat. "I remember that paneling. It used to be all over the place."

Alan smiled. "Yes. We've removed most of it, but my little office still seems stuck in the eighties." His eyes narrowed. "You've visited our club before? That's interesting."

She straightened the hem of her black plaid skirt. "Yes. My parents were members here."

Alan looked again at Anna. "Hmmm. I've been here for twenty years. You do look familiar."

"I was much younger then. My family left Redbird Creek about ten years ago."

He snapped his fingers. "That must be it. You would have been a teenager when you were last here." He smiled, but a look of confusion crossed his face followed by a moment of silence. "If you're a former member, may I ask why you want to work here?"

Anna clutched the broken heel of her shoe. She'd been expecting this question. "Why not? I grew up in this club, and well, it's like coming home for me. If you look at my resume, you'll see I'm an experienced event coordinator and worked for a club in New York. They were thrilled with my work."

Anna placed the resume on his desk and noticed a few creases on the paper from her unsteady walk into the office. She attempted to smooth the paper, but it was useless.

Alan pulled out a pair of reading glasses and perused the resume. "It seems you achieved quite the career there. Weddings, anniversary parties, even dances. Have you ever planned a golf tournament?"

"Not exactly, but I did help with the catering end of one."

He looked up suddenly. "So, why did they let you go?"

When you don't want to answer a question, keep it vague, Anna remembered her father saying. "I needed a change."

Alan leaned his head slightly to the left. "A change? Somehow, I think there's more to it. You left New York, one of the pre-eminent event centers of the country, and returned to Redbird Creek, Texas, where the beef-and-beans day at the county fair is still the social event of the season." He ran his finger along the page. "I assume you won't object to me calling Mrs. Samson at the Whispering Pines Club?"

"I wouldn't mind at all, except she passed away since I worked there."

He pinched his lips together, making the tiny mustache protrude slightly, like a caterpillar on a juicy leaf. "That's unfortunate. Well, I'm sure there's somebody there who—"

There was a knock behind Anna. "Alan," the voice spoke on the other side of the door, "I need your opinion."

Alan took the resume and aligned it with the corner of his dark green desk blotter. "That will be our chef," he told Anna. He looked toward the door and raised his voice. "Give me a minute. I'll be right there."

He returned his gaze to the resume and then to Anna. "I know I should take more time to check out your references and, trust me, I will, but you've arrived at a very busy time here at the club. The yearly tournament is coming up. Our last planner left abruptly, and there's still so much to be done." He exhaled. "I take it you can start immediately?"

Anna gulped. "Yes. Of course."

"Good." Alan gazed at the broken heel in Anna's hand. "And buy a new pair of shoes before you come back."

"Yes, sir." Anna rose and, grabbing her things, limped to the door. Upon opening it, she nearly ran into a broad chest, the hands in front holding a plate of cupcakes.

"I'm sorry. Excuse me." Anna tried to step out of the way but forgot about her missing heel and stumbled back.

"Anna? Anna Holman?"

Anna looked up. One thing about your past—even though it was supposed to stay buried, it had a way of coming back when least expected. "Yes."

"It's me. Caleb. Caleb Armstrong. Remember me?"

Anna looked into the eyes of the bearer of the most delicious-looking cupcakes she had ever seen. Her stomach grumbled. Not the grumble easily hidden with a cough, but a grumble that alerted people for miles around.

"Would you like a cupcake? Nothing like cupcakes between old friends."

"Thanks." Setting her portfolio down in a chair, Anna grabbed one, peeled back the paper and took a bite, letting her teeth sink into a mixture of chocolate, butter, and ecstasy. She swallowed. She remembered the tall football player who always had one of her friends on his arm. "Yes. It's nice to see you, Caleb."

"You two know each other?" Alan asked.

"We went to high school together. We were kitchen buddies in Home EC class," Caleb said.

"Too bad none of that cooking stuff stuck with me," Anna muttered between bites. "Obviously, it took with you. These are delicious. Better than delicious. Incredible."

"Too much chocolate?"

Anna was savoring the richness. "No such thing. These are perfect."

"Great." He handed a cupcake to Alan. Anna couldn't figure out why she was so happy when he turned to her. "I didn't know you'd returned—"

Alan interrupted. "Chef Caleb, as much as I'm enjoying this little reunion, I agree with Anna. These cupcakes are wonderful, but as you can see, I'm very busy. You can woo our new event planner another time."

Anna wondered if she should leave. She'd been officially hired, and Alan's attention was now switching to the kitchen business.

There was a swift, deep flash from Caleb's dark blue eyes. It unnerved Anna so much, she looked away.

"Nice to see you again, Anna."

Anna nodded and crumpled up the cupcake wrapper. Caleb Armstrong was a name from her past, but he was also working for the club. Maybe she wasn't the only one to have a reversal of fortune?

"Oh, and Alan, I hate to tell you this, but we need to change our fish vendor," Caleb said. "I know he's your cousin, but if we want to get some decent shrimp for the shrimp remoulade, we'll have to use someone else. Also, I need to get your approval on some menus for the upcoming tournament."

Alan gave Caleb a smile. "Well, Hal isn't going to like it, but if you want to go with someone else, I'll smooth over the waters. Go ahead."

Caleb nodded, glanced quickly at Anna but, after a second, returned his gaze to Alan. "I'd like to give Beamer Fish a try."

"Whatever. As far as the menus for the tournament, you'll be pleased to hear I've hired Anna here. She'll be our new event planner and the one who'll be in charge of those decisions. Thank God."

An overwhelming feeling zinged through Anna as it suddenly hit her. She was jumping from interview to job in seconds. It happened so quickly, she felt unprepared. She was told she would be planning a golf tournament but didn't have any connections to the tradesmen in town like she had in New York. Anna tried to convince herself she was equipped to do this. Contributing to her panic was the realization she'd be working with Caleb, a man who still thought of her as Anna of Redbird Creek High. She wasn't that girl anymore. She stole a glance his way, only to be mortified to realize he was looking at her. Anna tried to get back to business and ignore the undercurrent between them. At least she sensed it on her side. Did he feel that little lightning bolt when he looked into her eyes, as well?

"Um, when do you want me to start, Mr. Partridge" Anna asked.

Alan raised a single eyebrow in astonishment. "Isn't it obvious? Today, if possible. If not, within the next twenty-four hours. And please, call me Alan. I'll show you where your desk is, and you can take a look at our previous event planner's files.

"Follow me and, Caleb, tag along." Anna's new boss motioned with his hand. "You need to know where you'll be taking your questions. One of the complaints of our former planner was being made to share an office in the back of the pro's shop. I hope I've remedied the situation."

Anna stepped forward, but so did Caleb. As she drew nearer to him, she caught a whiff of cupcakes and vanilla.

He bumped into her elbow. "I'm sorry." He placed a gentle hand on her arm. "Please, ladies first."

Anna stepped in front of him, trying not to inhale the heavenly scent of baking.

Gladys stood from her seat when they returned to the lobby. The foot traffic had picked up as more tanned tennis players breezed in with towels around their necks. A mixture of sweat and expensive cologne mingled to create an odor of rich, casual living.

"Excuthe me," Gladys sniffled, her *s* coming out as a *th* sound. "Is my interview next?"

"Oh, yes. Gladys." Alan addressed Gladys as if an afterthought. Something most people did with her. "I've just hired Miss Holman as our new event planner. If you're still interested in a job, we can use you as Miss Holman's assistant. A failsafe for the club until I get her references validated. Although you were a cordial cashier, checking people out in the grocery isn't even close to event planning."

Gladys gazed at him, then, like watching a tennis match, she looked at Anna then switched to Caleb. She bobbed her eyebrows up and smiled, only to change gears as she stifled an unexpected sneeze. From behind a tissue she muttered, "I'll take it."

Alan's lip curled as Gladys blew a honk loud enough to quiet the lobby for a second. "Wise girl. We're walking to the office you'll share with Anna. Come along."

Caleb fell in step with Anna as she limped along and placed a hand under her elbow to help steady her uneven walk. Anna was thankful for the help, if not a little unnerved by his closeness.

Gladys took up the cause on the other side. "I had a pair of Walmart shoes break. Sometimes cheap is too cheap."

"You think?" At first, she wanted to snarl, the response she previously gave Gladys in the old days, but somehow she didn't. She hadn't meant to sound so mean, but somehow, this place brought the mean girl out in her. She needed to remind herself she wasn't that girl anymore. She quickly backtracked. "Sorry."

"No problem," Gladys snorted. "Having your shoe break in a job interview is pretty tough sledding. I'm pretty graceful, so it's never happened to me, but you know what I mean."

Anna eyed Caleb, who was quietly listening. From his amused look, Anna guessed he appreciated Gladys's view on the world.

"I'm surprised you work here as a..." Anna struggled for words. He was basically a laborer. Blue collar. One of those men in the kitchen she ignored every day she'd been at this club.

Caleb's grin spread slowly. "Kitchen help? Yeah. I guess I never amounted to much."

"I'm sure you tried." The words shot out before she had the chance to take them back. She was like an alcoholic visiting a favorite bar. It would be hard not to drink or, in her case, let her mean girl flag fly. "What I mean is, there's no shame in hard work. I'm sure you do a splendid job."

"Thank you, your highness," Caleb whispered under his breath. His change in demeanor demonstrated he didn't appreciate her evaluation of him or his life.

After a trip down a dark hallway Anna didn't know existed, they came to a plain white door next to the ladies' room. It looked more like a supply closet than an office. Her new boss opened the door and flipped on the light.

"Here we are." Alan pointed to a desk in a corner sharing space with boxes of tennis balls and several tall flags with the words Redbird Creek Country Club printed on them. He pointed to a lone tan metal filing cabinet. "You'll find files on other events in there going all the way back to the sixties." There was a mixture of relief and gratefulness on Alan's face. It was obvious he intended to dump his biggest problem on Anna and move on. "I'll leave you to it."

Once Alan was down the hall, Anna kicked off her shoes and set her purse and portfolio down. She attempted to lift a box of copy paper off the desk, but Caleb was suddenly behind her.

"Let me." He stepped in and lifted it for her. Gladys cleared a counter next to the copy machine.

Caleb set the box on the floor and, crossing his arms, glanced back at Anna. "Welcome to the staff."

"Kind of a surprise hiring, but I'll take it." Anna took a breath. This was all happening so fast.

"Shoo." Gladys drew a hand across her forehead as if she'd just finished a grueling 5k. "Me either. I guess Alan has a good eye for talent. Strike while the iron is hot. All that stuff."

Caleb leaned against the counter, also known as Gladys's new desk. There was a note of curiosity in his voice. "So, Anna Holman, what brings you back here? I thought you were off in New York making it big. Living the high life."

Anna sat down, the chair squeaking loud enough to rouse a sleeping bear. "Not quite living the high life. I don't know. Maybe I got homesick."

Gladys, as though wanting to copy everything Anna did, pulled out a folding chair and pushed it under the copy machine counter. Her chair didn't squeak, but there was a peculiar air-passing sound as her bottom settled into the seat cushion.

Once the hissing stopped, Gladys looked at Anna. "I thought you were a part of the idle rich. You know, people who only work because you're bored."

There it was. How long was it going to take for the people in this town to not picture her as someone who took afternoon swims in her money vault? Should she come clean or try to focus them on the new Anna? She settled on the latter. "Well, there's only so much idleness one can take before it turns into boredom. I did a lot of event planning for my father and it naturally turned into a career."

"Are you back in the old house?" Caleb asked. "Remember the party you gave our senior year? I came with Wendy. Boy, what a night. Your old man always bought the best booze. I can still remember the hangover, which makes me glad I don't drink like that anymore. I guess there's a reason why we're only eighteen for a year."

Anna remembered the party, but not for the reasons Caleb did. Her father bought the liquor on purpose. It never occurred to him he was encouraging underage drinking. He wanted those kids to drink and if they got drunk, he would be there to see them home safely because he was such a good dad. It was another way to bond with parents he secretly saw as potential investors. If you trusted a man with an emotionally immature teenager, why not trust him with your life savings?

"Actually, I'm staying at The Corner Bend Inn. I haven't found a place yet."

"The Corner Bend Inn?" Caleb raised a curious eyebrow and paused. "A little plain for you, isn't it?"

Anna opened up the desk drawer to see the previous occupant left her an eraser and a pack of Juicy Fruit gum. "Well, it's what I can afford right now, and it's clean and comfortable."

"I think it's a lovely hotel," Gladys added. "My grandma always stays there when she's fed up with my mother. It *is* clean and comfortable."

To Gladys, any hotel was a step up from living in a double wide with family members crowded into every corner.

Caleb nodded. "Yeah, that clean and comfortable thing hits all the online reviews. I don't want to get into your business, but I know my sister, Jenny, has an empty apartment."

"Jenny?" Anna didn't even know Caleb had a sister. Was she older or younger than him? She didn't know much about Caleb, only what Wendy told her and the other girls. It was hard to imagine what Caleb Armstrong's sister would be like.

"Maybe you don't remember her. She came to my games, but she was always running around with a pack of kids. Tiny kid with pigtails with all the stuffed animals. Her room looked like a scene out of *E.T.*"

Anna gave a weak smile. "Vaguely." She still didn't remember her, although she did remember a group of sticky-faced children who spent most of the game running back and forth to the concession stand.

"Yeah, well, now she collects other people's animals. She runs a doggy daycare and lives in one of two apartments above it. Calls it Barkington Palace."

If the place was crawling with dogs, the rent had to be reasonable. Anna was already down to her last thousand dollars so overpaying for rent would leave her with the choice of eating or not eating. She thought she'd saved enough to make a move over a thousand miles, but she didn't figure on the cost of getting there and buying a used car.

"Really? It sounds like something that might interest me. Where is this doggie daycare?"

"Pearl Street, right next to the library." Caleb glanced at his watch. "If you like, I can take you over there in about an hour. I can reintroduce you and drop off some leftover bones for the pups."

Anna thought about the houses around the library. There was a stately old white house with an enormous yard on one side and a park newly built on the other. "Is it the old Wilder house?"

"That's the one. She's fixed it up and fenced in the yard so her children—what she calls them—can play."

Anna wasn't sure about living above a bunch of dogs, but she couldn't afford to be too choosy. Besides, she liked dogs but never found the time to have a dog in New York. It might be fun. "Thanks. I'd appreciate your help."

"If this works out, I'll be thanking you," he returned quickly. "The old lady who used to live in the apartment was deaf, so she didn't mind the barking. Jenny hasn't been able to find anyone else fool enough to live there. I know she could use the rent money."

"This is great news. I was worried about finding a place on such short notice. I guess my days at The Corner Bend Inn are numbered. Oh, and thanks for the cupcake."

"We cookin' folk have a heart of gold." Caleb gave her a sideways grin and winked. "See you in an hour, and I'll wait anxiously to hear why you're really here."

After Caleb stepped into the hallway, Anna blew out a breath she didn't realize she'd been holding. She remembered him now. It was suddenly quiet in the room as Gladys stared at her and grinned.

Gladys gave a quiet whistle under her breath. "He's cute. Do you suppose he might like someone with allergies?"

The next chapter in Anna's life had just begun. Working with Goopy Gladys. What would McKinzie say when she found out? Anna decided the best thing to do was concentrate on work. It would only be an hour before Caleb would be back to take her to his sister's house.

"Let's start digging around and see what's here to tell us how to plan a golf tournament. I don't suppose you've ever done anything like this?"

"Does a Putt-Putt party count?" Gladys asked.

"No."

Anna, not wanting to waste any time, pulled out a file marked "Golf Tournament." She hoped it would be all they needed. Anna anticipated lists of contacts, notes on what worked, player schedules, luncheon menus, and budgeting records. Instead, there was only a single trifold brochure from a past tournament. Clearly her predecessor wasn't much on record keeping.

"Look at this." Anna placed the near-empty folder on the counter in front of Gladys.

Gladys's eyes widened at the single document. "Oh, a brochure might be helpful."

"In what way? All we know is it happened, not how it happened. I wasn't in town during this time. Do you remember anything about it?"

Gladys fidgeted. "Not really. I remember a poster in the grocery store window. My family isn't the country club type."

Once again, Anna hadn't realized not everyone in town enjoyed life at the country club. "Sorry. The store where you worked as a cashier?"

"Yes, before that I worked in a convenience store and before that I kept other people's kids."

"You didn't go to college?"

Gladys snorted. "No money for college. I lived on a different side of town than you. I thought you'd know that."

Anna pulled her chair up next to her new assistant. She'd made an assumption about Goopy Gladys—she assumed everyone went to college after high school. Anna, herself, only attended one semester of college. It was the year her family moved from Texas to New York. She hadn't even declared a major before she dropped out and her father convinced her to forget college and help him with his business dealings. Anna suddenly realized she had a kinship with Gladys. Neither of them held a college degree, but she wasn't sure if she was ready to share it with Gladys yet.

"Right. I'm sorry."

As they looked through the brochure, Anna noticed Wendy Moorefield listed in the thank you section. Her mind flashed to Wendy and Caleb standing on a football field being paraded as homecoming king and queen. Wendy was queen of everything back in those days. The leader of her girl pack might show a friendly side one minute and be vicious the next. How had a person like Caleb ever dated her?

"I wonder what they were thanking her for." Anna pointed to Wendy's name.

"She probably donated a pile of money or something. Nothing like having your name on the donor list to show how important you are. The word was she was pretty disappointed in her first husband's social status."

"Who was hubby number one?"

"Caleb. You didn't know? They lasted for a year and a half before she divorced him, or did he divorce her? Can't remember. They looked good together, like celebrities on the cover of *US Magazine*, but I've never seen two people more mismatched. She's all about being seen, being popular. Caleb's more grounded. He loves his job, his family. You know the type." She gave a little sigh.

"Really?" Anna's mind drifted back to their close encounter. The undercurrent rippled back through her. She'd never felt anything around him when he was with Wendy. Not that she didn't notice him, but she didn't believe in going after somebody else's boyfriend.

"Well, whatever happened in Caleb's love life isn't going to help us now." Anna looked around the office, her plan for the tournament beginning to form in her mind. "Okay, I want you to start making us a resource file. Names, numbers, websites, emails. We need to set up a real folder for this tournament."

"I like the sound of that." Gladys's voice was a little nasally, but her excitement was almost too much.

Gladys was a notorious hanger-on in the past. Anna sadly wondered if she would spend the rest of her life listening to her new office mate blow her nose. She could have done this job anywhere else and succeeded and maybe even been happy. Something brought her back to Redbird Creek, yet she wasn't sure what it was. It was if she were meant to come here.

"I'll tell you one thing—Caleb really gets my motor going. He's so handsome." Gladys placed her hand on her scrawny neck, her gaze floating up to the ceiling.

"I'll bet he's taken. His kind always is. Plenty of good looks and rich women running after him." Rubbing her ankle, Anna moved her chair back to the desk and put all thoughts of Caleb out of her head. She opened the portfolio she'd brought for the job interview and pulled out a legal pad. Looking for a pen, she opened a side drawer in the desk and found a dog-eared employee handbook. Time to study up on Redbird Country Club, from the staff side, not as the spoiled girl her daddy raised.

Chapter 2

Caleb couldn't get over Anna had returned to Redbird Creek. He hadn't thought about her in years. He remembered her sitting across the table in one of the model kitchens in their home economics class. Her dark blond hair was cut to the shoulders now. She still had the curls, but it was shorter. Her light hazel eyes were amazing, and the way her lips moved into a smile was hypnotic.

Back then, his girlfriend Wendy went into a dramatic pout when it was decided they wouldn't be stirring up any muffin batter together. "I'm a little miffed you let yourself get into a kitchen group assignment without me," she had grumbled to him.

"It wasn't really my choice." He'd tried to intercept yet another impending temper tantrum. Wendy threw a lot of tantrums in those days. She was the most popular girl in school and Caleb counted himself lucky, but, at times, her sense of entitlement overshadowed her beauty.

"Fine," she poked out a bottom lip. "I hope everything burns. At least I have Anna in your group, so I'll know if you're making eyes at anyone else." Caleb had no desire to stray and was sure as beautiful as his girlfriend was, her insecurities were hidden behind bullying.

Caleb had liked home economics, something he didn't readily share with the rest of the football team. It was more than muffins. It was science. After all, cooking was mixing different substances with an expected outcome. He always liked to cook at home and was sure he was the only high school quarterback who collected cookbooks. He was eager to learn new things.

Their first cooking assignment had been chocolate cupcakes, something he loved to eat. Anna, Wendy's designated spy, had been a part of a group of girls his girlfriend hung around with in the hallways. One day in class, Wendy had pulled her compact out to touch up her makeup. He'd watched her as she angled the mirror and reapplied a coat of foundation.

Anna had followed his gaze. "There she goes again. She's going to get makeup in the food."

Caleb remembered turning to face Anna. "I'm surprised you aren't fixing your makeup. I thought you girls did everything the same."

Anna's eyes had twinkled. "You'd be amazed how different we really are."

He thought little of her statement at the time. The fact he remembered it now made it important somehow, but that was a decade and a failed marriage ago.

The only woman he saw consistently after the divorce was McKinzie Carmichael, but she wasn't the right woman either. Yes, she was manipulative, but available and, so far, she was never as awful as Wendy. He was settling because it was easy.

Anna's smile came back to him. There was something about it. It was genuine. Caleb tried to put away the thought. The last thing he needed was to get mixed up with another member of Wendy's pack of vicious women. He was better off with an enjoyable book and a pot of soup on the stove.

But he couldn't stop thinking about Anna. The way she tucked a stray curl behind her ear and gave a quick smile haunted him. As hard as he tried to put her out of his mind, there was something about Anna difficult to put his finger on, but he would figure it out. With his history of making mistakes with women, this time he would be cautious.

Fool me once, shame on you. Fool me twice, shame on me.

His interaction with her that day had been brief, but he was convinced she was purposely being vague, dodging questions. Whatever her secret was—if there was one—he was about to uncover it. He needed to be around her more and working together would make it possible. The problem was, he was certain the more he was around her, the more she'd be on his mind. His heart gave a tug. Why did it even matter to him?

The words rolled back through his memory.

"You'd be amazed how different we really are."

Chapter 3

Anna pulled her car up behind Caleb's at Barkington Palace, formerly known as the Wilder house. He leaned on the hood of his car, waiting for her, and smiled as she exited her own vehicle. At the club, she'd been so distracted by Alan's abrupt job offer and her broken shoe, she hadn't really studied Caleb. He'd been one of the best-looking guys in their high school—one of those jocks who develops a beer gut and receding hairline by his thirties. But not Caleb. He was maturing quite handsomely. Anna caught herself staring and quickly shifted her focus to the house. The green shutters had been repainted a schoolhouse red. A sign planted in the freshly cut lawn sported a giant black paw and whimsically advised dog owners to clean up after their beloved pets. Looking up to the second story, Anna noticed white curtains dancing in large windows flanking each side of a set of French doors, which led out to a pristine balcony inviting you to come and sit a spell. Maybe it wouldn't be too bad to live above a pack of dogs.

"What do you think?" Caleb asked as they mounted the wooden steps of the porch spanning the front of the Barkington Palace.

The brown coir doormat at the front door said: "Dogs Welcome. People Tolerated."

Anna bit her bottom lip as she surveyed the porch. It was as she remembered, but somehow, with the healthy green ferns and hanging porch swing to the left of them, it seemed homier. "I don't know yet. The outside looks good."

"Jenny's done a wonderful job with this place. It's her little piece of heaven on earth, although you wouldn't catch me living in a boarding house for dogs. Still, it's what she loves." Caleb opened the door for Anna and followed her into the foyer.

She liked the way Caleb spoke with pride about his sister. Anna never had a sibling and, considering all she endured with her father, another child might have taken some pressure off her.

"Are you talking about me again?" Jenny Armstrong flicked back a long, brown braid as she came down the stairs. Once at the bottom she put her hands in the pockets of her jeans. She was younger than Caleb and bore the Armstrong family resemblance. She had deep brown eyes, and her nose was slightly turned up. Next to her was a square-shaped Basset Hound with deep-set eyes and ears hitting near the bottom of his short legs. He sniffed at Anna's leg like she was going through security at the airport.

Caleb reached down and petted the dog. "I was simply telling your prospective boarder a little about you. She needs to know she's not moving in with a crazy woman."

Anna extended her hand. "Hi. I'm Anna Holman."

Jenny gave a knowing look. "No need to introduce yourself. I remember you. One of Wendy the witch's cronies back in the day."

"Ex-crony now. Wendy and I travel in different circles these days."

Caleb and Jenny exchanged a glance, causing Anna to worry she might have overstepped a line. She'd consider what she was saying before she spoke. It was one thing for the sister of a divorced brother to make a joke about his ex but another for her to do it.

"Good observation. Glad to know whose side you're on." Jenny smiled.

"I wasn't really taking a side." Still unsure, she figured she needed to stay neutral. Like Switzerland or vanilla ice cream. Anna wasn't so sure she wanted to take a side against anyone in this town. At least not yet. She wasn't there to get caught up in the local feuds, only to plan events for these people.

"Yes, you were." There was a friendly twinkle in Jenny's eye. "Come on in and let me show you around." The sound of barking rose in the back of the house. "They get excited when they hear my voice," she shouted over the din. "Do you like dogs?"

Anna did like dogs, but the howling in the background was a little unnerving. "I guess so."

"Good enough." Jenny led them upstairs, where the dog noise lessened considerably.

Jenny showed them the various rooms, and after the tour was over, she put both hands in the air and turned in the lovely area leading out to the balcony. "Well, that's it. A bedroom, bath, and kitchenette/living room. Are you interested?"

The upstairs reflected the same homey feel of the front porch. The décor wasn't magazine-cover level, but it was warm and comfortable. Even with the dogs downstairs, Anna was sure she'd sleep well here. It was safe here, tucked away from her father's world. It wasn't Fifth Avenue, but it was what she wanted in this new life. "It's perfect."

"Really? I mean, compared to where you used to live, it's kind of...cheap."

"You've done a beautiful job making this a home and a business. Besides, I don't know if Caleb told you this, but cheap is what I'm looking for right now. I'm lucky he told me about this place."

Caleb stepped forward. "You know, there are those apartments over on Redbird Drive. They have fireplaces and balconies, security—"

"And they cost an arm and a leg. I need you to understand I'm not the same Anna Holman living off her father's money. I'm making my own living, like you."

Caleb nodded as his lips curved up slightly. He was looking at her closely, and it made her uncomfortable, but he simply stated, "Well, that's different."

"And you're sure you can put up with the dogs?" Jenny asked.

"Sure."

"Good. How about barking, howling, whining, and maybe a flea now and again?" Jenny clenched her teeth in an "excuse me" smile, as if these things were a closely guarded secret until now.

"It's all fine. I know you've been having trouble renting this place, but honestly, you're a life saver. Your rent works for me. I've always admired this house, and now I'm actually going to get to live here."

Jenny put a hand over her heart. "I know, right? I love it here. It was high time I moved out of Mom and Dad's. Having two older brothers can be a bit life-limiting." She issued a sideways glance toward Caleb.

Anna was warmed at the brother-sister exchange. "You mean they wouldn't let you have any fun?"

"Basically. So, the way the daycare works is the dogs spend the day here, but all go home at night, except for my dog Jasper." She pointed to the Basset Hound, who was panting at their feet. He took his time pulling his bulk up the stairs.

"During the day, I train the dogs and give them exercise, a nap, and food. It's like a regular daycare, except my children are dogs. Will you be all right with it?"

Seeing as Anna would be away from the apartment most days, this wouldn't be an issue. "No problem. When can I move in?"

"Right now, if you're ready."

"Wow, when you two make up your mind, there's no stopping you." Caleb turned to Anna. "Welcome to the family," he stumbled with his words. "Or should I say, welcome to my sister's house. I guess we'll be seeing a lot of each other now."

"Guess so." Anna's face heated. *Why is this something to blush about?*

Jenny looked from Caleb to Anna and grinned. "If I may ask, what were you doing before this?"

"I was an event planner in New York." Anna's gaze drifted to the floor. She hoped to leave it at giving them a job description. Let them form their own story of her background.

After a few seconds, Jenny filled in the silence. "So, you're going to be working at the country club with Caleb?"

"Yes. I guess I am. It surprised me to see him working there as a…"

"Chef? Has he told you about his culinary school? My big brother is the real deal when it comes to preparing food."

Now Caleb blushed. "Enough, little sister."

Jenny gave a playful push to his shoulder. "He's also extremely humble."

A humble man. Something Anna didn't have a lot of experience with.

Chapter 4

Twenty-four hours later, Caleb came in a side door of the meeting room at Redbird Creek Country Club and joined Anna and Gladys at a long conference table. Their reflections mirrored them in the blacktop, which had been shined to the hilt by a member of the janitorial staff. "Is this where the help sits?" he whispered, drawing close enough for him to smell Anna's light vanilla perfume. If one thing would attract a chef, it was the smell of vanilla.

He noted a slight tremble in Anna's smile. She looked nervous. It was amazing Alan expected her to make a presentation the second day on the job. No stress there. He touched her hand, and she trembled a little. "Well, are you ready to present your ideas for the tournament? They sure didn't give you a lot of time."

"Ready as we'll ever be, I guess." She pulled her hand away. Was she nervous about the presentation or was it from his touch? He had to admit, there was a jolt of electricity between them. He tried to shift his focus back on the meeting.

Several older ladies were gathered closely together on the other end of the table. The elongated oak framed windows featured views of the ninth hole where brightly clad golfers went up and down the path in their golf carts. McKinzie was focused on her phone as she sat next to her mother, Mimi Carmichael. McKinzie set the phone down and gave Caleb a sultry look. He looked away before she had the chance to pat the seat next to her for him to join her.

On one side of the table a few older gentlemen Caleb secretly labeled as golf nuts were engaged in a conversation about a hole in one on the fourteenth hole. They played the course every day, whether it was so hot golf balls melted or so rainy golf carts had to be pulled out of the mud.

Alan stood at one end of the table. "Ladies and gentlemen." He gave a nod to the golf nuts. "I'm excited to share with you I've hired a new event coordinator, a former member of the country club, Anna Holman."

There were a few smiles and nods. One of their own was always welcome. It had to be good because it meant they were more likely to accept her in her new role as someone who worked *for* them rather than someone who was *one of them*. Caleb never had to make that transition, and he was thankful. His parents spent their Sundays at worship and not on the golf links. He would always be a visitor in their world, but marrying Wendy earned him social status. But his marriage to Wendy cost him things, too. Like a lot of Sunday dinners with his family and the weekly renewal he gained from studying God's word and being around a congregation who cared for him. After the divorce he happily stepped back to the working side of the club and rejoined his church family like a prodigal son. He'd rather be working in his kitchen than hitting a little white ball across the grass any day. As he watched Anna, he realized there was something different about her. It was as if she didn't feel she fit in anymore with these established families.

"And now, Anna, I know you've been working hard." Alan extended a hand in her direction. "Can you share your ideas for the tournament?"

Caleb clapped, "Go get 'em, Anna," and gave her a gentle push.

It was playful and sweet, but when Caleb looked over at McKinzie, his harmless endearment hadn't gone unnoticed. McKinzie wrapped her nails around the sparkling back of her phone with a frown. She was a beautiful, rich, single woman, and Caleb admitted to himself it was easy to fall back into familiar patterns from high school. It didn't mean they were exclusive. They'd gone on a few dates, sure. Nothing more.

Anna rose to polite applause. "Yes, it's so nice to see all of you again." She flicked on a projector she borrowed from the pro shop. "Here are some facts, figures, and ideas I'm sure will put this year's tournament over the top."

When Anna finished her presentation, which detailed plans for the tournament schedule, teams, food, costs, and registration, the room was quiet. "Any questions?"

McKinzie's hand shot up, her lips drawn into a line. "Anna, this is a lot to take in. May I ask what kind of experience you have in doing this kind of thing? I mean, is there actually a major in college for event planning? Didn't you drop out of college?"

Anna stiffened. "Yes, I did. Good of you to remember, McKinzie."

McKinzie straightened and gave a wry smile at Anna's compliment. McKinzie's claws were out. Why would she do that to someone she used to call a friend? With McKinzie you never knew if she was going to like you on any given day.

"I worked as an event planner, mostly for my father, in New York. I helped him host dinners, banquets, and even some weddings for some of his clients."

Mimi's hand went up. The older woman had a square figure and arms with no noticeable flab, a sure sign of one who kept themselves busy with sports, like tennis and golf. This club was her life and her body noticeably benefitted from it. Caleb guessed Mimi would likely live well into her nineties.

"So, why did you stop working for your father?" Mimi asked.

Caleb kind of wanted to know the answer himself.

"I hardly see what my father has to do with your golf tournament, but I decided I wanted to branch out and do a job I know full-time in my own hometown. I guess I missed it here."

"Isn't it wonderful?" Mimi brought her hands together over her heart. "She missed us."

"So sweet," Caleb chirped from behind Anna.

Anna blushed. Caleb was amazed at McKinzie's mounting anger. Her lips had thinned into a line and she looked like she'd bitten into a lemon slice.

"Seriously? We're taking a chance on Anna here," McKinzie said. "She says she's done all this...planning, but what proof do we have?"

"That's cold," Caleb murmured. McKinzie was full throttle going after Anna.

Alan stepped in to rescue Anna. "Don't worry, McKinzie. I'm checking her references. She has already shown tremendous organization and initiative. As long as it doesn't rain, I'm sure Anna and her team will do a stellar job with our long-awaited tournament. I say we give Anna a big Redbird Creek Country Club welcome."

There were a few nods and more clapping, but McKinzie sat with her arms folded.

As the crowd left, Caleb stood, and McKinzie joined him, putting her arm around his shoulders. Her focus zeroed in on Anna. "Looks like you have it all figured out. I'm not sure if I'm so keen on it, but you never know. They're pretty desperate." Even though she was delivering bad news, McKinzie looked happy about her observation. She tightened her grip around him.

"Tell me you did more than just your father's friends' weddings," Caleb added. "Redbird Creek might be a small town, but they don't know it. You, of all people, should know they'll throw you out in a heartbeat."

Anna blushed. "I can assure you I did more than a few weddings. I worked as an event planner at a club in New York. One, I might add, that was a lot nicer than this one."

Caleb was confused. Why hadn't Anna mentioned this before? "Why didn't you say that in front of them?"

McKinzie put a hand over her mouth and let out a little laugh. Not enough to be rude, but enough to be heard. "Could it be, the great Anna Holman was a little nervous?"

Anna raised her chin in defiance. It was obvious to Caleb she would not let McKinzie get under her skin. "No, of course not. Living in a small town, you may not realize how full my life was working in a city.

Also, the concept of working may be foreign to you, with your lifelong support from Daddy."

She was more than willing to stand up for herself. He liked that in a woman.

"I'm sure I don't know what you're talking about," McKinzie shot back. "I'm very involved in projects around the community. I strongly believe in helping the less fortunate."

Gladys, watching the whole scene, butted in, her chest extended slightly. "Anna worked hard on her PowerPoint. I did the graphics. Did you like them?"

Caleb smiled, his gaze never leaving Anna. "They were great, Gladys. Weren't they great, McKinzie? Who knew all those years ago, while you and your friends were busy managing the high school fashion police, little Anna here was dreaming of becoming an independent businesswoman?"

"For sure." Gladys's nasal tone dragged out the last word.

"Whatever." McKinzie turned away from Anna and Gladys and focused on Caleb. "Take me to lunch, Caleb. I'm starving."

Chapter 5

As McKinzie forcefully guided Caleb out of the conference room, Gladys turned to Anna. "He likes you."

Anna gathered up her computer and handouts. "Don't be silly."

Gladys shook her head from side to side. "I may not have a tremendous amount of experience in the dating world, but I've seen enough romantic comedies on Netflix to know that look. Caleb likes you. I'll bet he asks you out, and soon."

"He can ask all he wants, but I'm not looking to get involved, especially with Wendy's ex-husband and McKinzie's current boyfriend. These people are looking for me to screw up and getting involved with him would only add fuel to the fire."

"Okay, but you have to admit, you kind of like him, too. Right?"

"Don't be silly. I barely noticed the man."

Gladys made a sideways grin with her chapped lips and sniffed. "Could have fooled me."

Once they returned to their shared office, Gladys pulled a sandwich out of her desk and unwrapped it. Taking a quick bite, she spoke through the gobs of peanut butter and bread. "Well, I'm glad that meeting is over. I was a little worried you wouldn't be able to pull the PowerPoint off. There's so much clicking to do, and you have to talk about it, too." She took a gulp and held up the sandwich. "Peanut butter. God's super food."

Anna was also relieved she'd made it through the presentation unscathed. She'd proved to herself she had the ability to interact with someone like McKinzie in this new role but, unlike in high school, planned to remain a good person. For the most part. In the old days, she would have gone for the jugular, belittling past tournaments, and over-inflating her own abilities. The "all show and no substance" way of life was now more her dad's style than hers. Anna sorted out the presentation materials. "One thing about event planning, it's not for the faint of heart. People want what they want. Did you get the figures on the banners? When we get the final go-ahead, which we will, we'll need to get them up soon."

"I'm working on it. This would have been much easier if the last person who did this had kept records." Gladys took a huge bite of her sandwich, causing her cheeks to bulge.

"Yes, it would, but, after today's meeting, I can now see why someone would go into a total meltdown, stack everything in the middle of the room, and hit it with lighter fluid. The crowd in the conference room should be on one of those talk shows. I thought they wanted a golf tournament, but it seemed they wanted to argue more."

Anna's cell phone on the desk rang, and Gladys looked over. Nick Holman was listed in bold print on the screen, and Anna covered it with her hand. "I need to take this. Could you give me a minute?"

"I guess."

As Gladys stepped out, Anna answered, "Hey. I didn't expect a call from you in the middle of the day. I thought they didn't let you call until after your shift."

"Yeah, well, I need to ask you a favor."

"Okay." Anna warily bit her bottom lip, waiting for whatever was on her father's mind today. This was typical. He would get a notion and assume everyone else around him would be honored to help him. It was part of the reason Anna escaped back to the familiar surroundings of Redbird Creek. She'd hoped he was through with this town.

"Yeah, I've been getting into painting here. My therapist says it's a way I can exorcise my demons. Whatever that means."

"Sounds great." Anna had never seen her father do any kind of craft. Possibly he was really being rehabilitated? As much as she hoped this was the case, she doubted it.

"Yeah, but the thing is, these canvasses are starting to stack up. You know, I won't be in this place forever. They're letting nonviolent offenders out all the time."

Anna didn't even remotely like the sound of the prison's release system. According to her schedule, there was at least another year—or, better said, she would be able to enjoy at least another year before she was forced to put up with him.

"I want to send my paintings to you, and I can't seem to find your address in New York. Can you tell me one more time?"

Anna froze. She had anticipated this moment would be coming but hadn't expected it so soon. There was no way to tell him she'd given up her apartment last month after falling behind on the rent. She was already sending part of her first check at the country club back to the landlord, hoping he didn't mind she'd fashioned herself a payment plan to erase the debt. She scrambled for an answer.

"Uh, believe it or not, I'm...staying with a friend right now, and I'm not sure what her address is. Can I call you back later with it?"

"Seriously? You don't know the address you're staying at? Some days I don't know about you, Anna. Too bad you had to move. That was a sweet place. What happened to your apartment?"

"Oh, you know. Neighbors. Some loud ones moved in, and I wasn't getting any sleep at night. Half the building has moved out. I needed to get out of there."

"Really? I always thought of it as such a quiet building when I lived there with you." Anna had trouble telling if her father was buying this excuse or not. Never kid a kidder and never con a con man.

"Well, things change. Uh, hey. Have to go. Great talking with you." Anna ended the call.

Eventually, she'd have to tell her father she was no longer living in New York. Thank God she was still using the same cell phone. He had no idea where she was, and for now, she wanted to keep it that way. Having him know she was back in Redbird Creek would only cause problems. One thing her father considered himself entitled to was telling her how to live her life and going back to a small city in Texas wasn't what he'd call upwardly mobile. For him it was all about having the next big thing and giving the appearance of a man the world would envy. He was a man who was, as they put it in Texas, all hat and no cattle. She remembered a time they met with a bank president. She was astonished someone with that level of experience would be consulting her father about finances. Her dad told her it was all about looking the part, even if you weren't the real thing. If you did it long enough, eventually you'd be the success you were projecting. He not only expected the same of her—he demanded it.

Anna needed to come up with a friend in New York. Unfortunately, the only one she thought of was Lenny, a guy who lived in her old building, which would never work.

"Can I come back in now?" The telltale odor of peanut butter surrounded Gladys.

"Yeah, sure."

"Who was on the phone?"

"Uh, just an old friend."

"Like a boyfriend?"

"Not quite." Anna turned off the screen on her phone and set it back on her desk. "Now, what should we print on the banners? 'Get lucky at the Redbird Country Club golf tournament?'"

"It might increase the attendance, but I don't think you should make promises you can't keep," Gladys noted dryly. "Oh, and you have a visitor." She pointed to a man in an apron with the Redbird Creek logo and the name "Mickey" stitched on his pocket.

He was as short as Gladys and the apron was tied around a wide middle. His stub nose and pronounced cheekbones reminded Anna of an animated pig she'd seen on television. His scowl indicated he wasn't too happy he'd been kept waiting.

"Mr. Armstrong wants you to come to the kitchen and try a dessert he plans to serve for the tournament lunch," Mickey said.

Anna hardly thought she needed to approve the menu. She'd learned long ago not to micromanage. "You know they have phones for that kind of thing."

The man rolled his eyes. "You're telling me? I have plenty to do besides being an errand boy for the so-called great culinary king. The boss told me I was to escort you personally and not take no for an answer."

"We're awfully busy here. Tell him anything he picks out will be fine."

The man took off his cap and dabbed at the sweat on his forehead. "He told me you would say that, and I was to demand you come to the kitchen to sample his work."

It was a surprise Chef Caleb was asking for her opinion, and it was funny because Caleb didn't seem the insecure type nor the kind of guy who wanted someone to hold his hand.

She rose from her desk as her cell phone rang. Anna's mother was calling this time. What was going on? Did her parents wake up this morning thinking they suddenly needed to chat with the daughter they typically ignored? "Give me a minute and I'll be right with you." She pushed the talk button on her cell. "Hi, Mom."

"Anna? Where on earth are you? I expect you to come to the christening for Marvin's granddaughter. She's not much to look at—has Marvin's nose—but the kid comes with a trust fund you can't imagine."

Anna's mother, Lillian Holman, recently took the plunge into matrimony for a second time, as if nearly drowning the first time hadn't scared her. Lillian was an opportunist, starting with her childhood where she was what they called new money. She was never accepted by others in her class and when she latched onto Anna's father and when they moved to Redbird Creek, she was finally accepted by the upper class. Some days living here was hard because their life was full of lies and deception. After witnessing her parents' marriage, Anna vowed she'd wiggle her toes in the water for a long, long time before taking any plunges. When she married, it would be for life and it would never be with someone like her father. She wanted someone she could trust and who would trust her. The crazy part of all of it was she wanted someone she could love. Sometimes it seemed like her parents' relationship was no more than a business deal. It was good for her father. It had never been good for her mother and it was rarely good for Anna.

"Oh, sorry. I guess I didn't get your invitation."

Lillian kept brief contact with her daughter these days, but when it came to something like a special occasion where she expected family to stand behind her, she was all in.

"Well, why wouldn't you? Have you stopped checking your mail? Really, Anna, sometimes you're so frustrating."

"When is the christening?"

"This weekend at the house. You can bring a date if you like. In fact, it would be better if you brought a date. I certainly wouldn't want to introduce you as Anna, my spinster daughter."

Anna tapped her fingernails on the desk. Spinster daughter. Her mother always was the queen of the obvious. According to her, Anna should have married by now, preferably to someone who showed up in the social columns. McKinzie wasn't the only one overdue for a husband, according to her mother's playbook. Why didn't her mother see her own matrimonial track record scared her daughter to death? Her first husband was a scam artist, and her second husband wasn't much better. This husband profited from other people's misery when they sued in court, whether the case had any merit. Yes, Lillian Holman had a talent for picking them.

Anna hedged. It was time to tell her mother the truth. "I hate to have to tell you this—"

Her mother cut her off, disappointment in her voice. "You can't get a date? Now, now, dear, surely you can find somebody."

"Even if I could get a date, which I can't, there's no way I can be there."

"Why ever not? You can't tell me there's something more important going on in your life. What have you been doing since your father went into prison, anyway? Getting the house rearranged to my liking has been quite a chore, but it's finally over, thank God. I've endured a lot of time around Marvin's family and now I'd like to have the support of my family. Namely you. Even if you don't have a man on your arm."

Anna cringed as her mother added on layers of guilt. "I'm no longer in New York."

"Not in New York? Where are you? Did I say you were allowed to leave the city without telling me?"

Anna clenched her fist at her side. Lillian chose to be in sparse contact since her first husband's embarrassing downfall landing him in jail and, until this minute, she hadn't bothered to track Anna down.

"I wasn't aware I needed your permission to leave the city. Last time I checked; I was a grown woman."

As Anna raised her voice at her mother, Gladys, who'd been silently working, made an enormous deal of grabbing her coffee cup and exiting.

"I'm aware of your age, although sometimes I wonder. It's just you're my daughter and most people's grown children tell them when they move. So... where are you living?"

"Redbird Creek."

"Excuse me? Why in heaven's name would you go back there? You'll die alone and lonely in Texas. Mark my words, Anna. Redbird Creek has no theater, no museums, and no culture. They don't even have a decent taxi service. It's like living in the dark ages. I thought I'd suffocate when I lived there. You're telling me you went back there *voluntarily*?"

It was true Redbird Creek boasted none of those things, but Anna wasn't looking for a place to satisfy her mother's criteria. She was looking for a place to call home—or at least the place she used to call home. She'd been happy here, even if her parents hadn't been. They'd always differed from everyone else, but now she was finding she differed from her parents. She was trying to become a better person. What did they say? *When you're finished changing, you're finished.*

Anna needed to make her mother realize the change occurring within her. "That was you. I kind of like it here. I always did. This is where I grew up. Redbird Creek is my home."

It had been a lonely morning in New York when she realized she was unhappy and feeling more alone than ever. Her father's demands no longer filled her days. She wasn't sure she had the ability to make it on her own and starkly realized how much she'd depended on his money to survive. Her bills began to pile up, but the job she'd procured as an event planner at Whispering Pines came nowhere near the salary she needed for her lower Manhattan apartment. She'd never before worried about covering rent because her father always had more than enough money. What she didn't understand was he depended equally on her. That was when she started to change into the Anna she was now. Knowing the position in the life she'd been living was ripped away by her father's criminal pursuits, she would never again live unaware of the place her money was coming from.

"Darling, we don't even have a house there anymore," her mother reminded her. "Where are you staying?"

"I'm staying in an apartment. You remember the old Wilder house?"

"By the library? Don't tell me they've made it into apartments?"

"Yes." Anna decided it would be wise to leave out the part about living over a pack of dogs.

"Well, at least you're in one of the better houses, even if you're only in part of it. Are you catching up with our friends at the club?"

"Yes, as a matter of fact, I am. I enjoyed a conversation with Mimi Carmichael the other day."

"How nice. Maybe you can find a husband in all those hayseeds."

"One can only hope, right? I might even press my overalls."

"Honestly, Anna, sometimes you have to move on. I certainly did and look where I am now." Lillian let out a little sigh. "There's no way you could fly out for the party?"

"No."

Anna had forgotten the kitchen worker who'd come to fetch her. He now stood in the doorway, his beefy arms crossed across his chest and a look of impatience between his brows. "Ma'am?" he growled under his breath.

Anna stood one more time. "I'm sorry, Mother. I have to go. Good luck with the party. I have to see a man about some dessert."

"What? What are you talking about? You're turning me down?"

Anna ended the call. Even with everything in their uneven and sometimes unhappy past, Anna loved her mother and hated to end the conversation on that note, but there was no other solution. She didn't have the time or the money to catch a plane and go to a christening at a moment's notice.

"I want to sample whatever Caleb's cooking," Gladys burst out, standing behind Mickey and looking like a child being left out of a treat.

"Come along." Anna motioned to Gladys and started for the door.

Chapter 6

As they approached the kitchen area, Caleb was standing at a series of long banquet tables covered in pristine white tablecloths. The smell of the club's evening fare was delightful, and Anna's stomach was grumbling. When she worked in New York, she always stopped at a bakery or deli on her way to work. She had yet to get into the habit of stopping anywhere in Redbird Creek. She breathed in again, taking in the aroma of meat cooked with onions. What a pleasant smell to have in her workplace. Caleb, who smiled as she drew closer, was zigzagging a chocolate sauce over a square of orange fluffy cake.

"Sorry it took me so long, Boss." Mickey rolled his eyes and jerked his head toward Anna and Gladys. "This one here took my time to gab with her mama." He pointed to Anna with a look of disdain.

Anna clenched her jaw and stated in a low tone, "I already apologized."

"And that's the way it is with you people." Mickey launched into a falsetto. "So sorry I wasted your time, but I'm so much more important." He added a hand swish for emphasis.

Caleb tilted his head in Mickey's direction. "Enough. I'm sure you have plenty to do."

The man grumbled and stomped through the swinging doors to the kitchen.

Caleb turned his attention to Anna. "I've been working on something new." He grabbed a fork from a silverware bin and cut off a bite of the springy cake to serve to Anna.

She leaned in and he placed the cake on her tongue. Anna's heart sped up in the intimacy of the gesture, but the mixture of chocolate and orange exploded on her tongue. How were two different tastes so delicious together? Gladys got a fork to cut off a bite to sample the cake. She portioned off half a slice and popped it into her mouth.

"Do you like it?" Caleb crossed his arms against his chest, and Anna couldn't help but notice the muscle tone under the bulging white chef's coat.

"I love it. I had no idea the high school quarterback had the same incredible talent as Rachel Ray!"

"Can I have another piece?" Gladys had a dot of chocolate sauce on her chin.

Caleb smiled. "Save a little for everybody else."

"I could eat the entire cake," Anna admitted. "I didn't eat breakfast. It's so good."

McKinzie came up and slipped her hand under Caleb's arm, pulling him close. Anna wondered if she'd been waiting in the wings, on guard. Talk about staking out one's territory.

"I'm not surprised. Caleb is a professional chef. The country club is just a stepping-off place. Someday he'll be running a kitchen in a four-star restaurant." As she gazed at Caleb, there was pure adoration in her eyes as if showing off a designer handbag. Caleb was going places whether he liked it or not.

"So, you say." Caleb put a stop to McKinzie's hero worship. "I'm happy right here, right now."

"You're so sweet, dear, and I know this will be perfect for the dessert after the tournament." Even though she only had eyes for Caleb, she tore herself away and faced Anna. "I'm glad you stopped by. Is there a chance we can get your dad here for the tournament? I mean, he was a silver-cup recipient, and we had the idea to honor our past winners at the closing night dinner. I probably shouldn't be telling you this, but you know I have such a big heart." She leaned in closer. "My mom and I were concerned after your little presentation. You haven't ever done something like this before and the last thing we want is for it to flop because of your inexperience. So, we came up with the idea of inviting past players. Great, right? Everyone would love to see him. If he wanted to, he might play a round of golf. Doesn't it sound like fun? It's going to be the best tournament ever, with our help, of course." She bobbed her head and gave a plastic grin.

"You forgot to say, 'and if it doesn't rain.' That's how everyone seems to be ending their sentences lately." The thought of coming up with another excuse made Anna's nerves rattle. How could she tell McKinzie her father wouldn't be playing a round because he was tied up in the prison laundry? "It's sweet of you to come up with this plan to protect me from failing, but I don't know. My dad is really busy."

McKinzie gave Anna a side look. "Ah, come on. You found your way back. I'm sure he can, too."

"I should probably get back to the kitchen." Caleb gazed at the door, his point of escape.

Anna gave a stiff smile. "I'll try to remember to ask him."

"Wonderful," McKinzie smiled, but there was a cold look in her eyes. "We haven't heard much about the Holman family around here. Whatever have you all been up to?"

Anna's gaze dropped to the floor. "Nothing out of the ordinary." She looked up at Caleb. "Excellent work on the dessert. I can tell working around you is going to be tough on my waistline."

Caleb's gaze roamed over Anna, centering on her face for a moment too long. "Just doing my job." He pulled his arm free from McKinzie.

"Will I see you later?" McKinzie drew her mouth into a little pout.

Caleb didn't answer at first, as if considering her offer. "Maybe."

McKinzie smiled and bit her bottom lip, looking so sexy, it was almost as if she'd been practicing in front of the mirror.

Before Anna had the chance to exit, McKinzie's gaze focused on her like a laser pointer. "You're not getting away that easily. You still haven't told us what happened to you. What has been happening at Casa de Holman, Anna? I was sure you'd be married by now with a couple of kids." Her gaze slid to Caleb. "Didn't you, Caleb? We thought you'd headed out to greener pastures, although I have no idea what's in New York you can't find right here in little ol' Redbird Creek."

Anna searched for a plausible answer to McKinzie's question. She couldn't tell her they'd gone to New York because her father left his job to search out a get-rich-quick scheme involving taking other people's money and sending out false investment statements. People like McKinzie never worried about money, and it would surprise her to know what Anna went through in New York. She wasn't about to tell her about when she discovered what her father was up to and how it shook her to the core. She had been so disgusted it was easy for her to separate herself from him when the police took him away. As hard as she tried, dealing with the guilt was nearly impossible. Even though she hadn't been aware of everything he was doing, she should have been less trusting of him. It was hard for a daughter to see her father as a criminal. Some days the guilt of her involvement crept back in, but today she needed to get McKinzie off the subject. She needed to come up with something that sounded right but not interesting enough to want to know more. McKinzie reinserted her arm under Caleb's.

"We went to New York to be closer to my aunt. She wasn't doing well, and you know how my family is. Always thinking of others." It was a lie, and Anna was ashamed how quickly it came to her lips.

Gladys nodded approvingly. "It's really nice of you guys to go all the way to New York to take care of your ailing aunt."

Caleb pulled away slightly. Not enough to insult McKinzie, but a stark contrast to the "we are a couple" pose. "You never told us you have family in New York."

"What can I say? This is Texas. I'm never quite sure how well it will go over." Anna thought of the salsa commercial where when the cowboys discovered it came from New York City, the first thing they said was "get a rope."

"Come, come now. We aren't complete snobs. You don't have to talk with a twang to be socially acceptable. We welcome New Yorkers, along with their checkbooks." McKinzie giggled to herself. "Why do you think dude ranches are so popular?" She narrowed in on Anna, like a hawk spotting a mouse in an open field. She turned to Caleb. "Don't you have to get back to work? Why don't you leave Anna and me alone so we can do some catching up?"

"You want to catch up with Anna?" Caleb looked a little surprised at her sudden interest in someone other than herself.

"I care about other people and their...lives." It was obvious McKinzie didn't care in the least about other people, but she tried to make it sound convincing and sealed the deal with a concerned look directed Anna's way.

"There's not much more to tell." Anna backed up slightly and folded her arms. "We moved up there to take care of my aunt and after a while, I came back here." Anna took a quick breath. "End of story."

Gladys went over to the squirt bottle containing the chocolate sauce and was preparing to squirt it directly down her throat, but Caleb quietly took it away from her. Not to be deterred, Gladys picked up the empty dessert plate and licked any remaining spots of chocolate.

McKinzie slanted her eyes slightly as a smile played on her lips. "Anna, dear, that can't be all there is to your story. It's been ten years. Where does your aunt live and why haven't you ever talked about her before?"

"Oh, she's very private. It took a lot for her to call us for help."

"So why didn't you hire one of those live-ins to stay with her? It hardly seems realistic to uproot your entire family."

"We've always been the giving type?" Anna's voice rose in a question on the last word.

"Your mother? The giving type? If I remember right, she gave my mother fits every time they worked together on a project. Lillian was famous for taking the lion's share of the credit for anything."

Anna had talked herself into a corner. If she told them her aunt died, they might question why her parents remained there. Which would create the need to come up with yet another lie to cover the first one. Anna glanced at her phone screen, clicking it on. "Look at the time. I have to get back to work."

McKinzie put a foot forward. "But what is your dear aunt's name?"

"Um."

"You can't remember her name?"

"Don't be silly. It's Janet. Aunt Janet."

"Janet what?"

Caleb asked McKinzie, "Why do you want to know?"

"I thought I might send her an invitation to our little tournament so she can see how her southern cousins live."

"I doubt it," Anna blurted. "She almost never goes out."

McKinzie smiled. "All the same. What is her full name?"

"Her name is," Anna's eyes strayed around the room, desperately trying to come up with a last name. "Her name is carpet... carpenter. Janet Carpenter."

"Like the old brother-sister singing group?" McKinzie snapped her fingers. "I'll be sure to remember that."

"Any relation to the singers?" Caleb asked.

"Distantly." Anna anticipated some questions when she reappeared in town—particularly from the country club set—but she never figured she would have to give names and concoct detailed stories. Anna was reminded McKinzie was one of those people who might seem nice at first because of her beauty, but cross her and she was deadly.

Anna grabbed Gladys's arm, forcing her to stop licking the plate. "Back to work, Gladys. Don't you have some reports for me to sign?"

"What? No..."

Anna widened her eyes in a glare of a desperate need for her to understand her.

"Uh...yes." Gladys nodded. "Reports. We're up to our ears in those things."

Chapter 7

That evening as Caleb drove up to his parents' house, he couldn't get Anna out of his mind. The more McKinzie questioned her today, the more evasive Anna became. She seemed to only be willing to discuss the present and avoid the past. Which could mean she was hiding something and based on the amount of squirming she was doing, adorable as it was, it was something she was worried about revealing.

"Caleb?" His mother, Beth, called out from the kitchen as he came through the screen door of the sprawling Texas-style ranch house.

"Hello, Mom." He reached the kitchen, leaned down, and kissed his mother on the cheek. "I didn't know if this was exactly what you wanted for the dinner, but I baked my cheesy bread to go with the spaghetti."

"It's perfect!" She clapped her hands. "Now grab a beer and sit down and tell me what's been going on in your life. I hardly ever have you here by yourself. When your brother and sister are here too, Jenny does all the talking so I never get fully caught up on what's going on with you. Besides, your father isn't home yet, and I'm needing a little company. Now I'm retired, I'm finding this house too quiet. It's not like working at the hospital, where I was surrounded by women who gossiped about everything."

"You should have had all girls."

"What's the fun in that?" She stirred the pot on the stove.

Caleb put a hand to his forehead and pushed back his hair. He drew out a sigh. "My life. Well, I can tell you one thing for sure. It's been interesting lately. Do you remember Anna Holman?"

"Friend of Wendy's?"

"Yes. She's come back to Redbird Creek and has taken the job as event planner at the club."

Beth raised an eyebrow. "And how do you feel about working with her?"

"I'm not sure. She's different somehow."

"How?"

"I'm trying to figure it out. She's the same old Anna, but she won't say much about her family. Did you know they moved to New York?"

"Really? I always wondered where they went." Beth set the spoon down and, picking up a glass of iced tea from the counter, pulled out a chair and joined her son.

"I guess Redbird Creek wasn't big enough for them. Her dad still works there. He must be really successful because Anna keeps talking about how busy he is."

Beth pursed her lips. "I completely forgot."

"What?" Caleb asked.

Beth left the table and went to her cluttered roll-top desk. Caleb's mother's filing system appeared to be a mess, but she claimed she could find anything in a minute or two. Sometimes it was better to not interfere in someone else's chaos. "I found it!"

Caleb rose and joined her at the desk. Beth had told him she liked it her desk was visible from the kitchen. She could cook and loved being able to work at her desk while things simmered.

"What?"

"My investment. I invested one thousand dollars with Mr. Holman years ago. It's amazing I forgot about this." She handed Caleb a tattered paper from one of the many cubby holes in the ancient desk.

Caleb read through the document. "Wow. You should have some money back on your investment by now."

"I should. Even though he moved, my money in those stocks never did. I wonder how I get my earnings?"

"I'll ask Anna if she can give us her father's new office number."

"What an unexpected blessing. This is like I contributed to a Christmas club account and I didn't have to do any scrimping." Beth's eyes glowed, and Caleb was happy for his mother. It was always nice to find a little extra money hidden away. Ten years' accrual on a thousand dollars wouldn't make her rich, but it would be some extra money she didn't have to work twelve-hour shifts for.

He would ask Anna about it immediately.

Chapter 8

The next morning Anna got the go-ahead on the golf tournament. She was digging through a closet looking for course signs when Caleb came up behind her.

"I heard they accepted your plan for the tournament. Congratulations." Today he didn't have on his trademark white chef's coat but wore a light blue button-down shirt and well-fitting khaki pants. She tried not to notice how the blue material stretched over his broad chest and how that made her feel.

He looked all business, but her mind drifted for a moment. She pictured him wearing this outfit on a date. A date with her. Anna tried to clear her thoughts. She was dealing with enough problems without fantasizing an evening out with Chef Caleb. Would he cook? Anna again tried to focus.

"Thanks." Anna wiped her brow. "Alan told me to dig out all the directional signs they used in other tournaments, but I had no idea these things would be so dusty."

"You should have asked Gladys to get the signs."

"I can't have Gladys do all the dirty work. It wouldn't be fair." Anna drew in a ragged breath trying to keep her focus on retrieving the signs and not on Caleb's chest.

"I want to ask you about something, if you have a minute."

"I always have a minute for Chef Caleb." Anna put down a sign and sat in a nearby chair. If he only knew how many minutes she would be willing to dedicate to him, he'd probably run the other way. Some days she was more like Gladys, with all her neediness, than she would ever admit.

"Good. I don't know if you are aware of this, but my mother invested a slight amount with your father years ago. I told her last night you'd come back to Redbird Creek and it reminded her about the investment. She'd completely forgotten about it. The thing is, she recently retired from the hospital and is taking stock of her affairs. Can you give me your dad's number so I can call and see about cashing it in for her?"

Anna's entire body went rigid. She hadn't known one of her dad's victims was right here in Redbird Creek. She'd assumed he didn't start the Ponzi scheme until a year after her parents' divorce. Caleb's mother was different from the other club mothers she'd grown up with, including her own. Where they had been judgmental, Caleb's mother was always kind. Beth was a sweet lady, and the thought of her father taking her money made Anna sick to her stomach.

"How much did she invest?" Anna hoped he would say an amount as small as a hundred dollars. Possibly she could attempt to pay it back. Much more and she'd be struggling. She wanted to make this right but wasn't sure if she would be able to in her current financial state.

Caleb watched her for a moment. "Not much. Only a thousand dollars, but to my mom, it was a pretty big investment."

"I'm sure it was."

"So, can I get his number?"

There was no way she would let him contact her dad. They only allowed prisoners to call out. "I'd be glad to call and find out for you. We talk pretty often."

"That's unnecessary. I'd rather handle this myself." Caleb paused, still waiting, but Anna didn't immediately answer. "There isn't a problem, is there? I mean, for her to cash in her investment?"

"Problem?" Anna gulped and tried to make her voice sound light. "No problem at all. I'll have it in your hands by the end of the week."

Caleb frowned. "Again, it's not necessary for you to get involved."

"I insist. I always liked your mom. Let me do this for her."

His expression softened a little. "I don't know why you're trying to fix this for your father, but okay, by the end of the week."

"No problem."

Anna gripped the edges of her chair. When would she ever stop hearing about her father's victims? He sat in a minimum-security prison, spending his days learning to paint and telling a counselor all his troubles, relatively untouched by the daily worries of people trying to scrape their lives together after he emptied their savings. Those bars kept him in but conveniently kept the consequences of his crimes out.

Chapter 9

Once again, Caleb was confused. Why was Anna being so secretive? Why would she not freely give out her father's office number? Had she always been like this and he hadn't noticed, or was it something more?

"Hope I'm not interrupting? I have wonderful news!" McKinzie wore a tan tank with matching slacks and exactly the right amount of gold jewelry.

"Come in. Not interrupting. Caleb and I were just finishing up," Anna motioned McKinzie in with her hand.

"Wonderful. I want you to hear this too." She winked at Caleb and looked around. "Where's Goopy?"

Caleb tried to stifle a laugh at McKinzie's lack of tact. Goopy was precisely the name that rose in the back of his head every time he looked at Gladys, and it was an effort to squelch it. Not so much for McKinzie. It wasn't right, and he needed to think of Gladys as an adult, not the butt of so many jokes from high school. He was trying to be a better man. The man God intended him to be.

Anna rose and returned to dusting off the directional signs. "Gladys asked for the afternoon off. Something about getting one of her mother's tattoos removed."

"God, I'd forgotten about Goopy's mother. She was even more of a character than Goopy. She's the only one I ever saw try to paint a doublewide. Life is funny, you know. You never know what might happen. My old friend is now stuck working in a pitiful little office with Goopy Gladys and the nose that never stops running at the country club where we used to hang out. Gladys's like the Energizer Bunny but for snot."

"Yes, it's a veritable laugh riot," Anna mumbled dryly.

Anna's office was small, but Caleb would never have called it pitiful. Not wanting to give McKinzie more chances to belittle, he tried to steer her back to the conversation at hand. "So, what's your big news?"

McKinzie pulled out her phone. "You know I've been trying to round up legacy players in our tournament. Do you remember Tad Silva? Remember that black hair and those dark eyes? Anyway, I found his contact information on Facebook. I asked him if he wanted to come back to Redbird Creek and play in the tournament. He's a talent agent now, out in California. Guess what?"

"What?" Anna echoed.

"He's coming... and... he's bringing *Little Michael*."

"As in Little Michael, the rap star?" Caleb asked.

"The one and only. You'd better get ready because wherever Little Michael goes, millions follow. Our golf tournament is about to be the biggest event this part of Texas has ever seen."

"Really?" Anna asked.

It was good news because if there was a record crowd, there was no way Alan would let Anna go. Caleb wasn't so sure why this felt right. He couldn't deny he there was something when she was around, but he still wasn't sure why she wouldn't tell them much about her time away.

Anna pulled free a sign from the stack she was working through and rubbed her nose with the back of her hand, leaving an adorable streak of dust across her cheek. "Wonderful. Thanks, McKinzie. It's quite an achievement you actually got us a celebrity."

"Well, I should confess I did it mostly for Caleb. He's a superb chef and cooking for Little Michael and his entourage might get him an important job out in California. I would l-o-v-e to live out in LA. Sometimes Redbird Creek can be so dull."

"Sounds like you have big plans for Caleb's future."

Caleb shook his head. "Thank you, I guess."

"Oh yes, darling. Even if you can't see working every angle is paramount, I'll do it for you. Mark my words. Someday you'll have one of those cooking shows and we'll go on book tours for your cookbook, appear on late-night TV..."

"Both of you?" Anna asked.

"Of course not. It will be Caleb. All Caleb. I never said both of us."

"Yes, you did," Caleb added.

"Oh, well, I mean I'll be the strong woman behind the successful man." McKinzie's phone serenaded them with a song from the Backstreet Boys. With a clank of gold jewelry, she held up the phone to read the screen. "This is interesting. A call from Wendy. Now I get to find out what she has been so quiet about. Back to the salt mines with you."

"Right. Thanks for the heads up on Little Michael, McKinzie," Anna said.

"I've always been abundantly helpful to those around me." She admitted it like it was some curse. She put the phone to her ear. "Wendy, where in the world have you been?"

McKinzie walked off in animated conversation and Anna touched Caleb's arm. "So, how do you feel about McKinzie planning your next career move?"

Caleb let out a sigh. "I try not to take McKinzie too seriously when she's on a roll like this. She can plan all she likes, but I'm pretty happy right here."

"Well, she might have done me a big favor getting a celebrity to attend my first event. Surely the attendance will pick back up. I'm not even sure who Little Michael is, but it doesn't mean anything. If McKinzie knows who he is, quite possibly other people do too."

"And what McKinzie says goes around here."

"Uh, thanks for not mentioning the thing about your mother to her. I really appreciate you keeping it quiet."

"Well, we still haven't spoken to your dad, so I don't see it as an issue...yet."

Chapter 10

When Anna re-entered the office, Gladys had not only come in on her afternoon off but sat in front of her computer on a website titled *Two Hearts Online Dating*. The women shared one computer and their work at the country club certainly didn't involve online dating. On the screen was what could only be described as a glamour shot of Goopy Gladys wearing a black feather boa and what looked like a sequin bustier.

"I thought you were taking the afternoon off. What about your mother's tattoo?"

"She decided to keep it. Frankly, between you and me, Dolly Parton's face looks wrong on her arm, but to each her own, I guess. I hope you don't mind, but I don't have a computer at home right now. The one I bought at the pawnshop started smoking. I should have bought the two-week guarantee. I'm almost done."

Anna looked at the screen. "Is that you?"

"Yes. I just had this taken. You can't fathom how hard it was to breathe because of all those stays."

Anna wasn't sure what Gladys deemed allowable but was sure she wouldn't be putting a picture of herself online in a bustier. "I don't know. This is like advertising. It's all about the message. Is this the message you want to be putting out there?"

"What message?"

"Uh, someone up for anything?"

Gladys bit her bottom lip as she stared at herself. "I want to have an exciting romantic date. I guess I am."

"You don't understand, Gladys. Someone might interpret it as *up for anything*. Anything being mostly sex."

Gladys gulped. "Sex?"

"Yes. Sex with a capital 'S.' Is that what you're interested in?"

"No. Well, yes, eventually, but I want to have a date first."

"So might someone else, but it might be a quick date, if you know what I mean."

Gladys clicked her mouse and deleted the picture. "I do. I guess I'll put back the old picture, but no one has answered me in months." She uploaded a second picture showing Gladys in one of her functional brown sweaters and glasses, her straight brown hair framing her face into an elongated oval. It wasn't as sexy as the first one, but it was a more honest representation of Gladys.

"Much better. Whatever made you get interested in online dating?" Anna asked.

"Everybody's doing it. We need to get your aunt Janet online. It will change her life."

Anna didn't like Gladys's plan for her mythical aunt, but Goopy was all ready to provide her with a handsome, digital man.

"I can do it for you. All I need is a recent photo of her. Do you have one on your phone?"

"Uh, no. She hates to have her picture taken. Besides, she really isn't interested. I talked to her, and she told me she was surprisingly happy not having any men in her life. So, thanks, but no thanks." Anna needed to get Gladys off the topic of Aunt Janet. It was all a lie, and it made her ashamed to repeat it—or worse, watch it grow. She'd seen her father do it and take advantage of the trust people put in him. Yet, since returning to Redbird Creek, she found herself manipulating the truth as skillfully as he had done when closing countless business deals. Now her little lies were turning into an ever-branching tree of lies.

"We need to set up the schedule for the tournament," Anna said. "Also, McKinzie told me Little Michael might attend. Isn't it great?"

Gladys clicked off the screen and bent slightly forward, mouth open. "Really? Wow! A real, live celebrity right here in Redbird Creek." She put both hands under her chin. "It's kismet." She spoke in a softer, dreamy voice, "He saw me across the green and there was a thrill of excitement cursing through my soul." She lowered her voice. "I was his woman."

Who needed cable when Gladys provided this entertainment?

After letting Gladys go home for the day, Anna closed the office door and called her mother. She'd been wrestling with what to do about replacing the funds for Beth's investment. She didn't have the money, but perhaps her mother would scrounge some up for her. Anna vowed she'd never take money from her parents again, but this was different.

"Yes, dear? This really isn't a good time. Marvin is filming one of his commercials. They're about to let the tiger out of the cage."

Anna's new stepfather was a lawyer who flooded the New York airways with his commercials, mainly shown between nighttime talk shows and late movies. His tagline was, "Marvin Simpson, a tigerrrr who will get your settlement." In real life, Marvin was a portly, balding man in his fifties who looked more like a walrus than a tiger.

"I wouldn't have called, but I'm running into a problem here, Mom. I'll be quick. I'm working at the country club."

"Working at the club? Doing what?"

"I'm an event planner, but that's not what I want to talk about right now. The people at the country club want to contact Dad about coming back to play at a tournament."

Lillian let out a little laugh on the other end. "Wouldn't they be surprised to find out he probably won't be free for another year?"

"One more thing. Caleb Armstrong's mother, Beth, made an investment with Dad and seeing me reminded them of it. They'd like to cash in their investment."

Her mother stopped laughing and took in a long breath and then blew it out. One thing Anna's father was good at was leaving a trail of victims that popped up occasionally.

Finally, Lillian spoke. "This isn't good news for you, dear. This was probably from the time he was getting started in Redbird Creek. He wasn't as good at covering his tracks in the beginning."

Her mother's words shocked her. Somehow, Anna had assumed her mother was as innocent in this as she was. "You knew about what he was doing, even back then?"

"Give me a break, Anna. Of course I did. There was no way he was paying our mortgage with his income selling cars. He was good at it, but not that good. He was still trying things out on a small scale. I'll bet he doesn't even remember making the deal."

"Yeah, well, he got lucky she forgot about it until now. But now my presence has reminded her, and her son is getting suspicious. What am I going to do?"

"If I were you, I would have a to-go bag packed and ready at all times in case you need to leave in the middle of the night. Do you know how much they invested?"

The thought of having to leave Redbird Creek in a hurry made Anna's heartbeat faster. "A thousand dollars. Do you think she's expecting gains off her investment?"

"Hopefully, you can make up something about a down market. See if you can get the paperwork. I'll try to send some cash. Marvin watches every penny, but I'll tell him I went shopping or something. I swear, I've never seen a rich man who spends so much time counting his money."

It was true. Marvin never wore anything but an off-the-rack suit, even though he was more than able to afford hand tailoring. He owned a beautiful home but turned off lights in every room except for the one they were in. He was the only millionaire Anna knew who clipped coupons.

"Can't say I blame him. Not everybody gets rich by conning little old ladies out of their retirement. Some people actually work for it, and they generally want to keep it," she told her mother.

"I'll see what I can do. You don't want your father to have the distinction of wrecking your former life and now your new one. After our discussion earlier about the lack of men in your life, we need to acknowledge not all of us can scrape up a new husband."

The part about men was an insult, but her willingness to help was one of the most touching things her mother ever said. "Really? You'll help me?"

"I'll be glad to do it for you, but if more suckers pop up, you're on your own. Marvin isn't dumb."

"Thanks, Mom."

"This old girl hasn't gotten so comfortable she can't handle a little scrambling to cover a con. You've got enough to do without them finding out their old financial expert is in the slammer for running a confidence scheme."

There was a light knock on the door and Caleb stepped in, papers in hand. Whatever he wanted, it didn't look good.

"Talk to you later, Mom."

Chapter 11

Caleb watched Anna stow away her phone. "We need to talk."

"Sure. What can I do for you?"

"I started looking at the stocks your father set up for my mom. There are some irregularities, and I'd like to discuss it with you. Do you have a minute?"

Anna shifted in her chair, causing it to squeak. Caleb wasn't sure, but she looked nervous.

He pulled a piece of paper from a file folder he'd been carrying. "I checked out a few of these investments your dad made for my mother and…I don't know what's going on here, but some of them don't even exist. I'm curious where your father came up with Sunburst Technical Innovations. I did some research, and there's never been a company of record with that name. Can you explain this?"

She bit the corner of her lip. "Well, no. This was my father's work, not mine. Could it be a misspelling or a typo?"

"Nope. Sunburst Technical Innovations isn't a real company, is it?" He narrowed his eyes, and Anna fidgeted.

She wasn't much of a poker player. She was hiding something. He was sure of it.

Caleb raised his chin slightly. "But maybe you were aware of it all along?" He slapped the folder shut. "You know, your family left town very quickly and the rest of us wrote it off to your father finding success elsewhere. We thought he might have been too big for Redbird Creek and possibly, that's what you wanted us to think."

Caleb took Anna's lack of response as a confirmation Sunburst Technical Innovations was a phony company. He feared if he dug deeper into the list, he might discover all the companies were fake. The fear and suspicion suddenly turned into anger. He sensed his blood pressure rising and his head pounding.

"So? What do you have to say about this? You know what I think? You took my mother's money. Unlike your parents, my folks had to work hard for their money, but along comes a slick customer like your father and poof—" Caleb made a starburst with his fingers. "He takes it all away with a smile and a sweet deal."

Anna cast her gaze downward. Had she herself perpetrated this con? "I don't know what to say."

"A quick call to the police department will get you talking plenty. I hope you have an excellent lawyer because you're going to need one." He pulled a cell phone from his pants pocket.

"Wait," Anna held up her hand. "I need you to realize what you're doing. If I become part of a police investigation, it will be the end of my job here and the end of my life in Redbird Creek. Wait a minute, okay. Please don't call the police."

Caleb moved his fingers over the tiny screen but soon he looked into Anna's pleading eyes and his frustration with her lost steam. "I'm willing to listen to your side of the story."

"Thank you, but I would appreciate if you kept this information to yourself. I haven't shared this with anyone in Redbird Creek."

"Not making any promises. I'd rather hear your story first," he said.

Anna's gaze rose and met Caleb's straight on for the first time since he'd entered the room. "You're right. My dad wasn't what he told people he was. I have no doubt he cheated your mom in an investment scandal. The money she invested is long gone."

"And there it is." His words were short and full of disgust.

"I know we gave the impression my family belonged as part of the upper class, but it turns out we were only visiting. Everything about us when I was growing up here in Redbird Creek was a sham. We didn't own our house. We were renting it. Those new cars my father drove around were loaners from the car lot. He convinced the owner the cars would fly off the lot if he was seen driving through town in them. You have to admit, he did look pretty good behind the wheel. Even the epic party I threw our senior year was all devised and manipulated by my father to get closer to the parents of my friends."

"Are you serious?"

"Sadly, yes. Of course, I didn't know it at the time. I was conned like the rest of you. I thought my dad made enough money to live like we did. When I found out differently, I decided to change my life. I don't lie. Or at least I try not to. I don't cheat people out of their money, and I'm trying to live a good life. Getting this job at the club was my lifeline. After everything my father did, I wanted, needed, to come home. I wanted to be in Redbird Creek even if the house I lived in was no longer ours and the way of life I was accustomed to was no longer achievable. Now, after all the craziness in New York, I've finally found some peace."

"Good for you, but it doesn't change the fact he cheated my mother out of her savings."

"No, it doesn't, but I'm working on getting her money back to her. I promise."

"And how will you manage to pay her?"

"I don't know, but she'll get her money back."

"So why isn't your dad fixing this?" Caleb raised an eyebrow. "Why do you have to clean up behind him? It doesn't seem right." It confused him why she would be so loyal to a man who was a criminal. Sure, he was her father, but it sounded like he caused no end of trouble in her life.

Before Caleb had the chance to continue, Anna stopped him. "He's in jail."

Caleb tried to speak over Anna, but mid-word took in a breath and blew it out. "Jail? In New York?"

"Yes. Your mom was small potatoes compared to all the other people and the amount of money he took from them. He didn't take as much as Bernie Madoff, but he did his fair share of damage. People trusted him. He had a way about him, you know. Handsome older man with silver gray hair who looked great playing tennis and, to top it off, gave you the bonus of a sensational stock tip. His game worked over and over again. Everyone trusted him."

"Like my mother."

"Exactly, and that's why I'm asking you to keep this to yourself. If people here find out I'm the daughter of a con man who used to operate in their circles, I'll lose my job. I need this."

"I don't know. I'm going to have to process all this."

Alan appeared in the doorway. "Anna? I need to speak with you."

Even though Caleb wanted to tell the world what Anna's father had done, something inside him hoped Alan hadn't been standing there long enough to hear anything.

Anna nodded. "Of course. Come in."

Alan slipped in, his upper lip twitching slightly. "Anna, I need to talk to you about these references—" He started to speak but instead locked gazes with Caleb, who stood squished behind the door.

"Caleb," he acknowledged.

"Mr. P," Caleb answered.

"I probably shouldn't say this in front of Caleb here, but it really is quite a trivial thing. I tried to call this Mrs. Webster up in New York, and she informed me you were working for her and suddenly, to her surprise, quit. Something about your father. I'm going to need more information. Illuminate me on the details of your sudden exit."

This wasn't a good day for Anna. The hits just kept on coming.

"Yes, well, it was a personal matter."

"Surely it can't be that personal," Alan added.

Anna's lips thinned and she shut her eyes tightly and, after a second, opened them again. It was if she was trying to transport herself out of the situation. "It was a family emergency. I'm not comfortable sharing much more."

"Anna, please. I'm trusting you with a lot of responsibility. Whatever it is, I'm sure it won't shock me. Trust me. I've heard it all." Alan gave Caleb a knowing look and a smile.

Anna stuttered. "Mrs. Webster was correct. It had to do with my dad."

Caleb doubted she'd tell him the truth. He waited to see what she came up with to appease Alan.

"What happened?" Alan asked.

"Yes, Anna, what happened?" Caleb echoed, playing the role of the concerned coworker.

Alan surveyed her. "I don't want to intrude into your family life, Anna, but I have to have some sort of reference to report back to the board. According to your resume, you worked for several years. Is there another reference?"

"I'll try to get you another name." Anna's lips thinned, but she sprang to a notepad on her desk. "Let me have you call Mrs. Simpson. Mrs. Marvin Simpson. I handled her granddaughter's christening."

"A christening?" Alan didn't look impressed.

"A New York City christening for a famous lawyer's granddaughter." She scribbled a number on the notepad and ripped it off. "Here's her number."

Alan took the paper hesitantly and eyed it. "And you're sure she'll give you a good reference?"

"I'm sure of it. Only give me a little time to let her know you'll be calling."

"Sure." Alan folded the piece of paper and put it in his pocket. "I'm glad you came up with another name."

"And so quickly," Caleb said. Anna wasn't fooling him. He was watching her pull a rabbit out of a hat to hide her secret.

"I'll give you an hour to straighten this out, and then I call this Mrs. Simpson."

"I'll get right on it. Thanks for your patience on this." Anna patted Alan on the arm.

When Alan left, Caleb listened for his footsteps, indicating their mutual boss had left the hallway. "Quite the performance, Anna."

She replaced the notepad on the desk as her gaze met his. She lifted her chin in a dismissive manner. "I'll work on getting your mother paid back. I promise."

He started to leave but, in an instant, turned back. "Get my mother's money and we'll be clear. After you've paid back her investment, your family and mine need never be in contact again."

Chapter 12

After Caleb left, Anna sent a quick text to her mother to tell her what to do. Once her mother confirmed she'd go along, Anna hoped she could somehow pull this off, but only if her mother came through with the money to pay back Beth Armstrong. If she could get through planning this first event, the people in the golf club would trust her, for the most part. She could pull in some side jobs, like birthday parties, anniversaries, and weddings. It would be wonderful to be making a living on her own, honestly, conning no one. It was what she thought she was doing when she worked with her father. This time she'd be sure of it.

When Anna arrived in her new apartment, Jenny, dressed in cutoffs, a Texas A&M T-shirt and her chestnut brown hair pulled back in a braid, was stirring a pot of chili in her kitchen. Jasper sat attentively by her heel watching her every move in case she dropped any on the floor.

"I hope you don't mind, but I used my key to get in. I figured after the hours you've been working, you might enjoy a home-cooked meal."

As Anna took in the aroma, she decided she didn't mind. "Is Jasper your assistant cook?"

Jasper's big brown eyes were turned upward in expectation. If Jenny moved an inch, his gaze was on her, probably where the coining of the word "watchdog" came from.

"Jasper is sure I can't live a moment without his presence. He has me on a firm five-foot ruling. I'm not allowed to get more than five feet from him, or he starts howling."

At the mention of the dog's name, Jasper's ears perked up. Anna bent down to pet the dog, scratching him lightly behind the ear.

"He loves you forever, now." Jenny gave Jasper a smile, and he wagged his tail.

Jasper's response warmed Anna's heart and, given the way she was feeling today, the basset hound could have qualified for a therapy dog. Her blood pressure was dropping with every wag.

Jenny observed her quietly. "Tough day?"

"Oh, yeah."

"I hope my brother isn't giving you grief. Ever since his divorce, he can't seem to stop himself getting into other people's business. I'm dating this guy right now who's a long-haul trucker. Immediately, Caleb tells me how truckers often lead double lives with wives and girlfriends in different towns. It's as if he can't get it through his head I can pick my own boyfriends. I know he's older than I am, but there comes a point where everyone is equal. Surprisingly, I've caught up to his stage of maturation as far as choosing someone to date."

"Sounds like Caleb. No, actually your brother was being pretty nice to me today." *Considering the fact he threatened to call the police and didn't.*

"Yeah, well he has his good days and bad." Jenny grabbed a wooden spoon and ladled some chili onto it. She took a quick taste and grabbed a second spoon from the drawer and offered it to Anna. "Taste this."

Anna dipped her spoon into the chili full of ground beef and deep red kidney beans. She wanted to taste it the minute she smelled it and when she did, she let out a sigh. "Delicious. Is this your own recipe?"

"It is. I love to cook, but I don't always have anyone to cook for. My last tenant loved my fried chicken."

"Well, consider me your future guinea pig. If all your food tastes like this, I'm in." As Anna spoke, her phone buzzed. It was a text from her mother. "Hold that thought." She pulled up the text.

You're in with your boss. I told him you were a fantastic event planner. Sorry, darling, but Marvin caught me trying to grab the thousand for Mrs. Armstrong. You'll have to come up with something else. At least I did one thing right.

Anna shook her head as she quickly deleted the text.

"I hope it isn't bad news."

"Uh, it might be." Anna thought about what she could sell to get the money to Caleb. There was her car, but Redbird Creek was too small to provide public transportation and her job was too far away to walk to. The blood center only gave you twenty-five dollars for a pint of blood. Not enough. Her options for fast cash were quickly running out. Her father would've come up with the money in only a few hours, but Anna was not her father. The kindness Jenny had showed her made the situation even tougher for Anna to handle. These were good people.

"Well, whatever it is, we're neighbors now, so if you need anything, feel free to ask."

Would Jenny be so kind if she found out about the debt owed to her mother? Her new housemate was sweet, almost like family. Too bad it was Jenny's family her father conned before he left town.

The next morning Anna was quickly running down a list of things to order with Eddie, the manager of the pro shop. Eddie had run the pro shop since Anna was a little girl and treated her no differently now than when she was a paying member of the club. For his simple kindness, Anna was grateful.

"I'm making sure I have extra staff on the day of the tournament for all of those last-minute purchases. Don't you worry about this order. I'll make sure it's in and on the front counter. After working with the last event planner, you're a pleasure to work with. What a loony. He didn't know if he was coming or going."

"Well, I can tell you he didn't keep records. We came into this with no resources and had to make contact all on our own," Anna confided.

"But you did it. Just goes to show we finally have the right person in the job." Eddie's confidence in her made her happy and a little nervous.

McKinzie came in, her face flushed with a healthy tan and the short skirt of her tennis outfit flapping in the breeze. "Well, Wendy has been found," she announced as if they had been standing there waiting for word from her. "Boy, do I have news." Her eyes glowed at the excitement of her secret.

"She was lost?" Anna asked.

"I saw you in here and had to run off the tennis court. I know I probably should've called the minute I found out, but one gets busy. Guess what? She didn't fall off the planet. She ran off to Vegas with her boyfriend last week and got married. That's Wendy for you. He didn't want to do the whole big wedding thing all over again. It wasn't a first marriage for him either. Our girl Wendy, who was desperate to land the only single doctor in town, even if he is a podiatrist, agreed to run off to Las Vegas and get hitched."

It was surprising Wendy would be satisfied with a Las Vegas wedding. She remembered in high school her old friend ruled as an imposing brunette who demanded everyone on the cheer squad have matching black sparkle shoelaces. When one girl told her she thought it looked silly, Wendy made sure she got kicked off the squad by telling the cheerleading coach she'd seen the girl smoking funny cigarettes by the bleachers. When Wendy wanted something, nothing would stop her. Of all the mean girls in all the towns, Wendy was the meanest.

A smiled danced on McKinzie's lips. "But there is a slight hitch in all of this. One, I'm afraid, will directly affect you, Anna."

"I haven't seen Wendy in years, and I don't even know the surviving single doctor in Redbird Creek, so how does this affect me?"

"The foot doctor told her she could throw a giant reception. She's already been on the phone to the caterer. I'm so excited because this will be quite the social occasion. Exactly what this dead-end town needs. Unfortunately, it's on the same day as the golf tournament. Which means anyone who's anyone will be at Wendy's party, not here."

Anna gripped the counter and tipped her head back in frustration. The world was spinning behind her eyelids. "I can't believe this is happening."

McKinzie snickered. "Too bad. Oh, and one more thing. Unfortunately, once word got out the tournament wouldn't be well-attended, Little Michael canceled. You know Todd Silva. If there's nothing to gain, he's out. It's probably the worst part for me, personally. I was sure this would be Caleb's big break. Guess this is a bad break for you too. If no one comes to your little tournament, I guess Alan will look for a new event planner. I'm sure Caleb will miss you. Then again, he's good at working with any old event planner. He was the only one who got along with the last guy, right, Eddie?"

Eddie smiled and didn't say a word.

This was exactly what McKinzie wanted. She could be a great friend, but only if things went her way. She was sure McKinzie targeted her because of Caleb. She leaned forward to test her theory.

"There's no way I'd let it happen, McKinzie. Not when I'm enjoying catching up with old friends, especially Caleb. You know, some people get better looking as they get older."

McKinzie pinched her lips together, creating a line under her nose that would someday be a wrinkle. "You're not his type."

"Maybe not, but I have reconnected with you—and even if you don't think we're compatible, I'm loving getting to know Caleb again. You know what they say? Nothing like a man in the kitchen to heat things up. So sexy in those chef's whites."

A storm cloud gathered above McKinzie as she reached out and placed her hand on Anna's bicep. "Listen here, Anna Bo-Banna." McKinzie squeezed. "Caleb is off the market." Her grip lightened a little. "You're kidding yourself if you thought he ever was available. Maybe you can hit on one of the cooks down at Denny's. Rumor has it they let them take home the extra food. Sort of a win-win for a poor little working girl."

"Really? Off the market? Are you guys officially engaged? I don't see a ring on your finger. After all, with you being twenty-eight and unmarried, you might want to rush things."

McKinzie's grip returned, making Anna wince. "I don't see a ring on your finger either. As painful as it might be for you, consider your own unmarried status before you criticize another's. At least I have a boyfriend."

Anna came right back. She flashed a gaze at her old friend. She wasn't going to let McKinzie get the upper hand. "I wouldn't be so sure if I were you."

Eddie put his elbows on the glass counter. "Enough, ladies."

McKinzie took her hand off Anna. She took a moment to regain her composure, running her hand along the hem of her tennis skirt.

Eddie gave Anna a friendly smile and then turned his gaze to McKinzie. "This is terrible news. Wendy must have known about the golf tournament. I'm sure I saw her new husband's name on the player list. What a shame after all the work Anna has done."

"Yes, it is a shame. But these things happen. So sorry for ruining your plans." McKinzie scrunched her nose and grinned. "There's always a chance this won't impact your little job, or your little assistant, Goopy Gladys. It'd be awful if you had to pack up and move back to wherever it is you've been hiding all these years. Did you speak to your dad about playing? He might draw a crowd coming back from New York and all."

"He can't make it." The words came out of Anna's mouth unexpectedly. She had planned a well-crafted lie to hide the truth of her father's incarceration. She never thought of saying no. The emotions of the moment clarified her thoughts and provided her with an answer.

"Really? Oh, well, but no worries. No one else will be here, anyway. Tah!"

As McKinzie left, a headache formed between Anna's temples.

"So, are we still ordering all this stuff?" Eddie asked from behind her.

"I don't know. I'll have to talk to Alan."

"Miss Wendy was like a bee to honey with that guy," Eddie mused. "She wanted to land him, whether or not he was married at the time, if you know what I mean. She kept telling him what a wonderful golfer he was. It was really hard to be quiet while she was talking. He hit every ball to the left. It was like golfing for NASCAR."

Anna gave Eddie a smile. Considering all this subterfuge, his honesty was refreshing. She was a coworker now, not a lady of the manor, and she was grateful for his kindness. As she made her way to Alan's office, her anger reignited. Had Wendy planned her reception on the day of the golf tournament or did McKinzie convince her to use that day? If Wendy and the doctor were already married, the reception could have been any Saturday. Why did it have to be her Saturday? Alan wasn't going to like this news. Anna felt a rush of guilt for wondering how to ruin the reception and not get caught. There was no way she'd let Wendy, and possibly McKinzie, get away with this.

"Anna?" Gladys stood in the hall, tissue in hand at her nose. "If the angry look on your face has to do with me not finishing up the menus, you don't need to worry. I'm done. Please don't be mad. My spelling has never been great, and I kept having arguments with the spellchecker. I'm really trying my best. I'm glad to be working with you. You're the first person from high school to ever really treat me like a friend, you know."

Her words stopped Anna cold. Were they so incredibly mean to little Gladys? She remembered some name calling she wasn't proud of now. She was trying not to be that girl anymore.

"It's okay. I'm not mad at you. I just found out Wendy has remarried and is planning a big wedding reception on the day of the golf tournament."

"Really? Oh no. Anybody who would be in our golf tournament will be going to her reception. This isn't good." Gladys's face dropped for a moment but suddenly, she smiled. "Life in a nutshell, isn't it? The married people don't care about what happens to the singles. Golf tournaments don't matter. Don't worry. We're in this together, girl. Sisters in pain. You haven't been married, have you?"

Anna prickled at her question. Why did anyone care whether she'd been married? She was tiring of having to answer for it. "No. I've never married." *Too busy trying to keep out of jail because of my dad.*

"If most people around here had to make a choice between a golf tournament or a fancy wedding reception, they'd choose the wedding reception. Free wedding cake."

"We've seen three cancelations for the tournament in the last half hour. I've heard about the wedding reception," Alan said from behind Anna. "This doesn't bode well for our finances."

"I was actually on my way to see you. What do we do?"

"That, my dear, is your job. Based on what you told me, Wendy was part of your crowd. Surely you must have some influence with her. I say you call her and ask her to change the date."

"With all due respect, she's not going to change it for me." Anna never had any influence over Wendy. Why would it start now?

Alan shook his head. "I guess you'll have to figure something else out and fast. We already have too many things ordered we can't return. Our budget isn't infinite. This isn't a big city club in New York."

"Can we move it to another weekend?" Anna pulled up a calendar on her phone where she listed all the activities the club would have in the next month. "How about bumping it to two weeks later?"

"Which will cause us to have to reprint a lot of promotional material unnecessarily," Alan frowned. "Did you have any idea this woman was going to schedule her reception on top of our tournament?"

"No. I'm really not in touch with these people anymore," Anna admitted.

"But you told me you were connected. If you truly had your finger on the pulse of the club, you would have known about this."

Alan was right. She had stretched the truth some, which made her wonder if she was still in the pattern of stretching the truth to get what she wanted. The apple wasn't falling far from the tree because it was something her father would have done.

"Sorry, but not even McKinzie heard about it until after the fact."

Alan put a hand on the side of his face and gave a slow shake. "I still feel like this was the kind of thing you should have known about. I'm not pleased. Not pleased at all."

Gladys, who had also taken out her phone, now jumped as she viewed the tiny screen. "Hey, your aunt Janet got hits on the Silver Fox dating site. She's really popular, especially since I put a picture of Helen Mirren in her profile."

"Excuse me?" Alan asked.

"Oops. I thought we were done talking about the tournament, right?" Gladys pulled her phone close to her.

"Am I to understand you've been using your time at work to set up Anna's aunt Janet on a dating website?" Alan asked.

"Maybe." Gladys poked out her bottom lip. If there were a poster girl for guilty, Gladys would be it, proving she would never be a good liar.

"That's it. First the tournament is a bust and now I find my newest hire is spending her time on dating sites instead of working." Without even taking a breath, he shouted, "You're fired, Gladys." He turned back to Anna, "And if you don't get this mess straightened out, you're fired too."

Gladys's face was like a souffle falling in on itself as Alan stomped away.

"But..." Gladys muttered after him. "I was only trying to help."

Anna put an arm around Gladys, who was now shaking. "He's upset about the tournament being upstaged by Wendy's wedding reception. Let me go talk to him."

"He fired me," she moaned, disbelief still in her voice.

"He was just angry, that's all. I'll bet he already regrets what he said. We can turn this around." Anna tried to comfort her.

"I quit my job at the supermarket where I scored a discount on Twinkies. Twinkies last forever. I thought I was moving up in the world. Now, they've probably hired somebody else. This is terrible."

"Okay." Anna looked over at the window and spied Alan getting into his practical blue Volvo. "He's leaving. Do you know where he lives? Maybe he's going home for lunch."

Gladys appeared to be stuck in the moment. "He fired me. Just like that. One day you're working in a posh club, like the Redbird Creek Country Club, and the next day scrubbing toilets at The Corner Bend Inn. No doubt where I'm headed. Toilets and sinks."

"Gladys." Anna shook her shoulders. "Snap out of it. Where does Alan live? Do you know?"

"I don't know, but he usually goes to my brother's bar right after work. Feeling the way he does, he might have gone there for lunch instead."

"Where's his bar?"

"You know, Sleepy Joe's over on Belmont."

"Wait, you have a brother who has a bar?" The Ledbetters couldn't afford to live in a house, but a family member was a business owner? Maybe one of them found success after all.

Gladys gave out a snort that turned into a laugh. "He works there, so I think of it as his bar."

"Sorry."

Gladys continued to laugh at Anna's assumption. "You work at the country club, but it doesn't mean you own it."

"Right. Well, seeing as my workload has been drastically cut for the rest of the day, I guess I'll head over to Sleepy Joe's for a drink." Anna reached in her desk for her purse.

"Please talk him out of firing me," Gladys begged. "Please, whatever you have to do. I'll owe you."

"You don't owe me anything. Let's just say I'm making up for all the mean things I did to you in high school."

Gladys looked a little confused but brightened up. It would take a lot more than this to make up for all the daily cruelty Anna and her friends heaped on Gladys.

"I'll buy him a drink and loosen him up a little."

"Do you want me to come with you?"

"No. I have this. And…thanks for trying to get my aunt Janet a date. I know you meant it as a kindness, but I need you to take it down."

"But why?"

"Even though to you dating sites are great, it doesn't mean other people are even close to being as comfortable as you are with the idea of dating a stranger."

"Okay, okay. I'll take it down, but I might take the world traveling proctologist for myself."

"Excuse me?"

"One of the eligible bachelors who wanted to meet your aunt Janet. He goes from country to country helping people in need. A shame to let someone like that get away."

Chapter 13

Caleb's mother sipped at her iced tea. "This had better be important. I have no idea why your brother was excited to talk to us and demanded we meet him here at Sleepy Joe's. I was supposed to meet my quilt ladies at the church. We've got to get a box ready to go to the mission."

Caleb sat at the bar next to his mother, his last conversation with Anna still swirling around his head.

"It's right next to the station. Pretty convenient if he gets a call. Believe it or not, I'm a little busy right now, too." Caleb immediately regretted his tone. He might be stewing over the situation with Anna, but he didn't need to take it out on his mother.

It didn't go unnoticed. "What's wrong with you today? You're as glum as a disorganized accountant on the fourteenth of April."

"Nothing." Even though he wanted to tell her, Anna was trusting him to wait. There was that word again. His mother trusted Anna's father with her hard-earned savings, but where did it get her? What would his father say when he found out? Trust was such an important thing, and when it was violated, it spoiled everything. He thought of a wall hanging his mother had stitched and hung in her kitchen when he was a small child.

Love cannot live where there is not trust.

~Edith Hamilton

He hadn't looked at it for years, but today the word "trust" beckoned to him. It seemed impossible to trust someone like Anna when she lied to him about her father's business. Trust was for chumps and a lot easier to stitch on a piece of cotton than to achieve in real life.

"Is something going on between you and McKinzie? Don't tell me she's trying to pressure you into marrying her."

Caleb gave her a scowl. "Please, we're barely dating. We've kissed once, and she was the one who started it."

"Who kissed you?" Sam barreled in as usual. The two men looked amazingly alike, except Sam sported dark curly hair cut short while Caleb's was blond with brown tones. They both had blue eyes, like their mother. Sam stopped and kissed his mother on the cheek.

"McKinzie," Caleb answered.

"Watch out. Those girls at the country club are all the marrying type. You got hooked once. Don't do it again." Sam pulled out a stool and took a seat at the bar. "I keep asking myself why you ever married a woman like Wendy. Actually, I was asking it on your wedding day but didn't want to spoil the mood," Sam joked.

Beth tipped her head to one side. "He married her because Wendy never gave him the option *not* to marry her."

"What's that supposed to mean?" Caleb asked as Sam signaled the bartender.

"My man, Gerard. Give me your finest ginger ale."

Now the wedding and divorce were over, it seemed Caleb's family was coming forth with some gentle truths about his relationship with Wendy.

Beth continued, "You went to culinary school, and she went to college. Even though she probably assumed college would be fertile ground for a husband, she came home with no man and practically demanded you marry her, and, for some reason, you said yes. We were all wondering what happened there."

"I don't know." Caleb stroked his chin. "Quite possibly it was the simple route." It was true. Caleb had always hoped God would show him who the right woman was for him, something dramatic like a sunbeam illuminating her as she walked into a room, but no sunbeams had reported for duty. Wendy showed up and seemed to be eager to marry him, so he figured she had to be the one. Why not? She was always the girl he dated in high school. It was comfortable and easy.

"Yeah, well, she came back as bossy as she was in high school. Maybe worse. When she started calling you Chef Caleb, I thought I'd die laughing."

Caleb reached out and thumped Sam on the head. "I liked that name."

Sam made a falsetto voice and brought his hands together over his chest. "Oh, Chef Caleb, you're so handsome."

Beth laughed. "Stop, you two. The past is the past, but now we need to move on. God only put one perfect person on this earth, and neither of you qualify." She turned her focus to Caleb. "You'll find the right woman someday. She'll be someone who fits in around here and doesn't put up with any of your guff. Whoever she is, I'll support your decision." She turned to Sam. "But first, Sam, why did you want us to meet you here today?"

"Because I wanted you to be the first to know. The captain promoted me this morning. I'm no longer a probationary fireman. It's official. I'm a fireman." He puffed out his chest.

Caleb put his hands together and copied his brother's earlier voice, "Oh, Fireman Sam."

"Yeah, well, at least my name rhymes," he joked.

"Congratulations! I know you've worked hard for this." Beth laughed at the antics of her sons. "I don't know what I'd do without you two goofballs in my life."

Caleb felt the same about her, except not the goofball part. "She's right. You deserve it. Congratulations," Caleb echoed.

"This is wonderful, absolutely wonderful." Beth glowed as she smiled at Sam. "Sometimes everything in life is perfect."

Even though she was having a perfect moment, Caleb needed to tell her about her lost investment, and this seemed like as good a time as any. "Mom..."

Beth's gaze closed in on him. "Yes?" Her eyebrows rose.

This was his big chance to make it right. He would tell his mother she had been swindled, and he planned to make it right for her.

He made a promise to Anna, and if he broke it, he'd be no better than the Holman family. He'd have to trust in the Lord to make it right. "Uh, nothing. I love you too."

Chapter 14

When Anna stepped inside Sleepy Joe's, she was greeted by the male version of Goopy Gladys. A man in his twenties, with the same widow's peak, rounded shoulders, and noticeable sniffle scurried up with a towel slung over his shoulder. "Can I help you?" Same nasal sound, only an octave lower.

Anna tried looking around in the semi-lit bar. "I was looking for someone."

"We all are, sweetie," he agreed solemnly. The man wore a name tag that read "Gerard."

"Yes, well, I'm looking for someone specific. His last name is Partridge?"

"Oh, him. He came stomping in here about ten minutes ago." Gerard pointed to a booth in the corner. "I'd be careful if I were you." He leaned a little closer. "Word of advice, I don't think he's *your* someone. My sister works for him, and she says he's a real stick in the mud."

Alan was in the booth, his hand against his temple, as if trying to rub away a headache. He had a tall dark beer in front of him, and he was already halfway through. This would not be easy. Drinking at lunch never signaled good things.

"He's my boss, too."

Gerard grinned. "Oh? You must work with my sister, Gladys."

"I did until a few minutes ago." It was bad enough she would have to beg Alan for Gladys's job back, but she hadn't counted on trying to explain it to her brother. Hopefully he would let it go.

"Oh, man, did he fire you?" Anna didn't have the time or the energy to get into this with Gerard. He'd find out about Gladys's job eventually, but it wasn't her responsibility to tell him.

Anna debated and decided to avoid the topic. "It wasn't me he fired. Excuse me."

As she made her way over to the booth, she noticed Caleb sitting at the bar with his mother. She never would've pegged Caleb as someone who would slip away to a bar for a quick beer. Was he telling his mother about her father's scheme to rid her of her money? Anna attempted to cut a wide path away from them.

"Mom—" Caleb looked away from Beth and spotted Anna. He straightened up and pulled himself off the barstool, gesturing for Anna to join them even despite her heading in another direction.

"Boy, do you have timing." He took her arm and directed her to where his family sat. "I'd like you to meet my mother. She invested some funds with your father once a long time ago." Caleb's eyes flashed dark blue as he spoke to Anna.

Beth extended a hand to Anna. "Nice to see you again, and do you remember my other son, Sam?"

"Nice to see you again." There was a resemblance between the two brothers in the cheekbones, noses, and those blue eyes. The older woman had the same dimple in her chin Caleb had, and her graying hair was styled in a no-nonsense blunt cut, falling a little below her ears. Beth still had her trim figure after three children. "So, you also represent the Holman Company? I didn't even know there was an office in town."

"There isn't. I'm Nick Holman's daughter, Anna. My dad lives in New York now."

Caleb's mother put a hand to her mouth. "I remember, or at least Caleb reminded me of it. How are you doing? I haven't seen you in years." She came off her barstool and embraced Anna, making her feel even more guilty than before. Would she be hugging her if she knew Anna belonged to a family who robbed her of a thousand dollars and called it an investment?

"What brings you back to Redbird Creek?" Beth asked.

"A job. I work with your son out at the country club, Mrs. Armstrong."

"Call me Beth." She directed her gaze to her son, who quietly sipped his drink. She gave Anna a gentle smile. "The last time I remember seeing you was at graduation, and you were with your group of girls."

"The same group, by the way, my dear brother seems to be dating his way through." Sam patted Caleb on the back.

Beth winked. "Hopefully, he won't be marrying his way through them as well."

Anna nodded as she noticed the more Caleb's mother talked, the more he blushed.

Beth continued, "How's your mother doing? I remember back in the day she was quite the Bunco player. Does she still play?"

Anna so wanted to answer her question but she needed to stay low profile, cards next to her chest, poker face at the ready. Her mother hated playing Bunco. She only did it because her father insisted. It was one thing to belong to the country club but another to wear silly hats and play a ridiculous game her mother had told Anna.

"I really don't know. She and my dad divorced and now she's remarried to a lawyer."

Beth's shoulders sunk for a moment. "That must have been tough for you. It seems marriages don't last the way they used to. I've been married to my Cyrus for over thirty years, and trust me, dear, there are times I wonder what life would be like if I was single again. Cyrus is a retired veterinarian and there are days when he prefers talking to his animals over me. He can be pretty frustrating when he wants to be, not unlike his sons here." She flashed a look to Caleb and Sam. "What's your dad doing? I suppose he's remarried too?"

Anna paused and her gaze met Caleb's. He was watching her closely, waiting for a slip of the tongue, and she was sure she would fail whatever test he had in store for her. Should she tell her the truth or make up a convincing lie? In the old days, this wouldn't have even been a question. She would have lied and said whatever she thought his mother wanted to hear. This was a skill she'd learned early on under the tutelage of Wendy and McKinzie, and later polished as she supported her father's efforts to rid people of their money. How much would it upset Beth to learn the person with whom she invested hard-earned savings was in prison for stealing from people like her? She struck Anna as a nice person, but, after encountering some of Caleb's moods, she couldn't be sure. Maybe Beth possessed a darker side, as well.

Beth leaned forward in anticipation.

Caleb took a long swallow of his drink.

Anna piped in, a little too quickly, "He's been busy with his job. He hasn't remarried."

"Of course. Your father always was very career minded. Well, if I remember right, he was quite the handsome devil. Looks, charm, and money. He won't be single for long."

Anna spotted Alan calling over a waitress. He would either order another drink or was asking for his check. Either way, she needed to talk to him about Gladys.

"If you'll excuse me." She made her way past Caleb and his mother, but before she could get too far, Caleb grabbed her arm.

"A minute of your time?" He guided her out of earshot of his mother, who was now speaking with Gerard and Sam.

He pulled her close to his chest. Anna's breathing was speeding up as he whispered into her ear, "What was all that about?"

"What was what?" she whispered back.

He pulled her closer and his breath tickled her neck. "You didn't tell her anything. You and your family can screw with anyone you want to in this town, but not my mother. She deserved to learn the truth from you, but you chose to keep her in the dark. I'll gladly tell her, and I still might, but I at least thought I would give you the chance to make it right with her. Obviously, my mistake. Return her investment or tell her the truth, and trust me, I'll make sure we avoid each other. Make this right."

"I know. You're right. I fully plan to pay her back. Don't flatter yourself. I wouldn't go near you even if you wanted me to. You won't intimidate me, Caleb Armstrong."

He gazed at her and a smile played on his lips. Was he smiling because he was attracted to her or feeling like he had the upper hand? Anna feared it was the latter—he was gaining power and she was losing it. She pulled her arm away as Beth looked over at them.

"Don't forget this moment and don't forget my mother and the trust she's putting in you." Caleb folded his arms across his chest.

"I'm sure you won't let me," she answered as she turned and walked toward the booth where Alan sat.

Alan was pulling bills out of his wallet as Anna approached.

"Alan, I wanted to talk to you about Gladys. Actually, I want to beg you not to fire her. She meant well and technically she was coming off a break."

Part of what Anna said was true. Gladys meant well trying to fix up her fictional aunt. Gladys always meant well. She was a people-pleaser, although she did seem to have a tendency to go off on a tangent and overdo it trying to please someone. Gladys never enjoyed the full acceptance of others, probably because half the time her face was behind a bunched-up tissue, but she meant well.

"I've made my decision, Anna. I need you to respect my authority." Alan lined up the bills in his wallet.

Anna noticed all the twenties faced the same way. This man liked order and precision, none of the things Gladys would ever be. She was sloppy, didn't know when to be quiet, and was way too needy for the average person.

Anna also couldn't help feeling Alan fired Gladys because she was the first problem to hit him after hearing their golf tournament was crashed by a quickie wedding and an over-the-top reception. It was a classic case of being in the wrong place at the wrong time. If Anna solved the problem of the golf tournament, she might save Gladys's job. She would start by buttering him up. It always worked for her dad.

She slid into the booth on the other side, putting both hands on the table in front of her. "I totally respect what you did. We can't have people on dating sites at work, but I need you to understand Gladys is a part of my team. She really digs in and works hard. She loves this job and will do anything to make the club a success."

Alan let out a "humph" as he pocketed his wallet. From the look on his face, he wasn't convinced. She talked a little faster, something she'd seen her dad do dozens of times. Flood them with reasons, he would say later. If one doesn't work, surely another one will.

"And exactly why I still need her if we're going to turn this golf tournament problem around."

Alan leaned forward and rubbed at his temple again. "And how do you propose we perform this magic?"

Anna was tossing around a crazy idea in her mind, but at this point it was her only solution. "Why don't we plan the tournament around the reception? If I can get Wendy to have it on Saturday night, when you would normally have the tournament dinner, her reception could be the featured event and we'll offer her the space free of charge. Knowing Wendy, she's probably having trouble finding a caterer for her reception. She can be very demanding."

Alan stopped rubbing his temple and his gaze met hers. She was getting through to him. "I'm listening."

Anna spoke quickly before he had the opportunity to change his mind. "I mean, where else is she going to find a space big enough and exclusive enough for her country club buddies, right?"

"Right."

"So, we have the tournament as planned. We tell everyone we're bending over backward to accommodate one of the club's most cherished members. People get to attend both events. As long as we have enough time for them to go home, shower, and change between the tournament and reception, they can do it. They'll want to do it. We provide a weekend they'll never forget and come out of it not losing any money. We get what we want, and she gets what she wants."

Alan stroked his chin. "You know, it might work."

Time for the zinger. Anna quickly added, "But only if I get to keep Gladys."

His bottom lip thinned. "Fine. You can keep Gladys but keep her and her tissues out of the way of the members. People are complaining about all the nose blowing she does. One of our hearing-impaired clients actually asked me why we have a foghorn in the club."

"Of course. I'll keep her in the background." Inside she was cheering. She'd done it. She'd saved Gladys's job.

"I guess it's settled...but..." Alan paused.

Anna didn't like the sound of this. Was he going to ask her to work for free or possibly not pay Gladys?

"...only if you get Wendy on board with all of this. Do you understand?"

"No problem." If only she felt as confident as she sounded. Convincing a woman to have her wedding reception at the tail end of a golf tournament wouldn't be easy.

Pulling up to the address in the club directory for Wendy's new husband, Reese Broussard, Anna steeled her courage. Fearing Wendy would be too busy to talk to her, Anna called ahead. Wendy's house was a generic red brick McMansion built on the edge of town in a subdivision which had popped up since Anna left Redbird Creek. Even though the price of these houses were surely exorbitant, she noted the homes were sometimes less than fifteen feet apart. It amazed her why someone would spend so much money on a house if the neighbor's bedroom window could clearly be seen from the adjacent house. If Anna was given the opportunity to choose a house, she would prefer to live in one like she was living in now. The cozy two-story home spoke of what a real home was. Jenny's house had a personality and, best of all, it was walking distance from the library. It was perfect.

The doorknocker was emboldened with a brass "B," and tall side cut-glass windows on either side of the door made the entrance to the home look elegant. Anna had never met this man, but if Wendy married him, she had a pretty good idea what type of man he was. He would be attractive, successful, and able to shut up when Wendy wanted to tell him what to do. The best word to describe Wendy was formidable. Worse, she was bossy, entitled, and drop-dead gorgeous. Anna wondered what Caleb ever saw in her. Why would he make such a giant error in judgment in the person he chose to be his bride? It proved what Anna was feeling about him right now. Sure, he was handsome, hardworking, and practically a boy scout. She also couldn't ignore the overwhelming rush making her a little dizzy when she was around him. He had a way of looking at her that made her feel like fairies were flying around in her stomach. But no. He was also a lousy judge of character, which meant it would never work. Never. Ever. At all.

Anna was surprised when Wendy answered the door herself. Her thick brown hair, full of body, glistened in the sunlight, undoubtedly the product of many conditioning treatments. Her hair was pulled back from her face and, even ten years later, Wendy was still stunning, but something about her looked different. Was it her nose? Yes, her nose looked smaller and squarer. Wendy had already ventured into plastic surgery.

"Wendy? So nice to see you again." Anna hoped Wendy wasn't picking up on the fact she was staring at her nose.

Wendy closed in for a cheek kiss. What was so interesting to Anna about this movement was although it was intimate, the participants never actually touched. A physical expression with no physicality.

"Come on in." Wendy led her into a white sitting room done with French Provincial furniture. "I'll get us some iced tea." She rang a little silver bell on the table and a woman in a blue dress with a white apron appeared. "Bring us some refreshments."

It was like a scene from *Downton Abbey,* but only with her old cheerleading friend as the lady of the house. If she were allowed to wander around the house on her own, would she find a kitchen with a wall full of labeled bell pulls?

Wendy turned her attention to Anna, who pushed a stray hair back into place. "It's wonderful to see you. I heard you were back in town—and working at the club." She whispered the last part as if it were an embarrassing fact, like trying to tell a friend she needed to freshen up her deodorant after a trying tennis match.

"Yes. I'm so happy." *Take that.* Anna might be working, but she was happy about it. No pitiful failure here. "And I hear congratulations are in order."

Wendy smiled and offered her a hand with a ring whose sheer size could launch a revolution. "Yes, yes. It was all spur of the moment, but you know how romance can carry you away." She stopped and adjusted her words. "Or maybe you don't." She gave her a thin smile. "Anyway, we flew off on Reese's jet and, next thing you know, I'm Mrs. Broussard."

"Sounds like a fairy tale, but actually, it's part of the reason I'm here today. I was wondering if you've booked a venue for your reception yet?"

Wendy looked surprised as she delicately dipped her chin. "We thought we would have it here. Reese has such lovely gardens."

Kept up by someone else. The flowers in front of his house were beautiful, and it would make a beautiful place for a wedding reception. If she planned to convince her and save Gladys's job, she'd have to use the hard-sell tactics of her father.

"Well, I wanted to make an offer on behalf of the club. Because you and Reese are long-time members of the club, we'd like to offer our dining room at no cost."

Wendy raised one expertly plucked eyebrow. "No cost? Seriously? As much as I appreciate your offer, we can afford to rent the dining room."

Anna realized her mistake. Wendy could afford the dining room rental. Offering it for free was an insult. She redirected her proposal.

"I know, but why put yourself to all the hassle? You can phone over your menu to Caleb, and he'll take care of you. Take all the worry out of the situation. We both know the hardest part of getting married is taking care of the loose ends. Caterers, florists, photographers, cakes. It never ends. This is what I do for a living now, and I'm surprisingly good at it. I would love to get the chance to show you."

"Yes, McKinzie has filled me in on you and your little career. That's the way she put it. Little career. She always was the meanest one among us. I don't mind telling you she's not happy about your coming back to Redbird Creek. What did you ever do to McKinzie, anyway? I haven't seen her on the warpath like this since the day I married Caleb."

Wendy's servant returned bearing a tray with two tall glasses of iced tea and a plate of cookies. She set it on the table silently and left the room. She was like a robot vacuum for drink service. Quiet and efficient.

Anna gently picked up a cookie. "Really? She didn't want you to marry Caleb?"

"No. McKinzie is always a bridesmaid, as they say. She attempted to go to the altar one time, but all I can tell you is it didn't work out. Maybe McKinzie will be the one who stays single all her life. You know the type, collects cats instead of men? What am I thinking? You, of all people, can relate. Word is you have no men on the horizon? I hear Goopy Gladys's brother, Gerard, is still available. You'd have to stock up on tissues, of course." She let out a shrill brief laugh.

"I've been too busy with my career to worry about trying to get a husband." The edge in Anna's words didn't seem to go unnoticed by Wendy.

Wendy's comments proved she was judging her old friend by her single status. Only here in Redbird Creek was this important. In New York, no one appeared to care about it, except for her mother, who repeatedly introduced her as her "spinster daughter" after Anna turned twenty-five.

"Yes, well. Marriage isn't always what it's cracked up to be. Neither you nor McKinzie would know what it can really be like. One day you're fine and the next day you wake up next to a person you can't imagine spending your life with. That won't happen with Reese. He's perfect for me."

Finally, Anna was hearing from the source about the problems between Wendy and Caleb. "Is that what happened between you and Caleb?"

Wendy pursed her lips, and her head gave a slight twitch. Anna hoped her actions meant she was breaking through her friend's well-polished facade.

"Caleb and I were only married for six months and yes, being married to a glorified cook, even if he was the quarterback in high school, is terribly dull. McKinzie can have him." She took a drink of her tea.

This was interesting, but Anna needed to get her back on track with the reception. "About your reception. We have a golf tournament going on the same weekend and, even though this sounds crazy, we'd like to make your reception a part of it. The guests who would be attending our tournament would also be most probably attend your wedding reception. This way your invitees aren't put in the difficult position of making a choice." Even though Wendy likely would not want to share her day with a golf tournament, Anna decided honesty was the best policy.

Wendy smiled. "Now I get it. You're trying to save your tournament."

"Yes, I am. I thought you would want to know the situation."

Wendy nibbled on a cookie. "Why would I? I know this is my second marriage, but I certainly don't want to have a secondhand reception where they pass out golf trophies."

Anna looked around the interior of the house and thought about her offer. There was no way Wendy would ever agree to sharing her glory with a bunch of sunburned golfers. She desperately needed to give her a reason to do it. Anna tried playing on the bond between them in the past. It wasn't a great friendship, but it was all she had. "The thing is, this is my first effort for the club, and it might go under if your reception takes away my players. I'm so happy to be back in Redbird Creek and getting to have all of you back in my life. There aren't any other event planner jobs in this town, so I'd not only lose a paycheck, but I'd lose all of you."

"Oh," she gave a little pout. "Poor Anna. Failing before she even begins."

And she said McKinzie was the meanest one.

The phone rang in the background and shortly the woman in the maid's uniform stepped into the room. "McKinzie on the phone for you, ma'am."

"Tell her I'll call her back."

"She says it's urgent, ma'am."

"Fine." Wendy reached over to an extension. "What is so urgent?" Some of the refined sweetness left her voice.

Anna remembered her tone from high school. The edges of McKinzie's voice were loud enough to come through the phone, and she didn't sound happy.

"As a matter of fact, she's here right now." Wendy listened to McKinzie and her lips thinned. From the clipped conversation and the increasing anger on Wendy's face, it was obvious there were unresolved issues between McKinzie and Wendy. Wendy finally broke into whatever McKinzie was saying. "Don't be silly. He's lucky to have you."

Wendy was silent, apparently listening to McKinzie. Finally, she let out an exasperated sigh. "Well...I've had a wonderful idea. I've decided we'll do the reception at the club instead. That way my guests can enjoy both events. Isn't it wonderful? I just came up with it."

Anna's heart skipped a beat as her old friend took the credit for her idea.

"Sorry, my news upsets you, McKinzie, but you'll get over it. Have to go. Anna and I have a lot of planning to do, and it gives us the opportunity to catch up on old times. Isn't it wonderful she's back?"

When Anna broke the news to Caleb later in the day, he was none too happy. He slammed the dishcloth down on the counter. "So, what you're telling me is on the day of the golf tournament, I need to switch gears and provide a dinner for my ex-wife and her brand-new husband? Seriously?"

Approaching Caleb with this wouldn't be easy, but his reaction went beyond what she expected.

"Do you realize how much planning a wedding dinner can take?" Caleb shouted.

Anna looked at him astounded. "First of all, it's a reception dinner, not a wedding dinner, and I definitely do after planning as many weddings as I have. I've been told I'm pretty good at this kind of thing, and I don't even have an ex-wife to show for it, like you do."

"After my brief time working with you, it's not surprising you don't have any old boyfriends in your past."

"What's that supposed to mean?"

"It's what's wrong with your entire group of vipers. Selfish people make lousy mates. Trust me, I found out firsthand and," he raised one hand, "as God is my witness, I'll never go there again."

"Don't worry. No one would have you, not with your attitude. No wonder I'm hearing complaints from your kitchen staff. You aren't a nice person anymore, are you? Has your unpleasant experience in romance soured you on the rest of the world?"

Caleb's cheeks reddened, and Anna wasn't sure how much further she should take this. Time to get down to business. "Listen, Gladys got fired, and this was the only way Alan would let me keep her. I know it's not ideal having to work for somebody you used to be married to, but I need you to work through this. Please consider doing this, Caleb. Now, about this dinner?"

He let out a lengthy sigh and pushed his shoulders back, accentuating a broad chest. "Do you have a menu?"

"Wendy gave me the one she was trying to get catered." Anna handed Caleb the menu, and as he read, a winsome smile crossed his features, and he shook his head.

"She *would* want crab claws. It's what she demanded we have at our wedding. As a matter of fact, almost everything on here is the same meal. Good old Wendy never did have much imagination."

"Can you do it?"

"With my eyes closed. Only, don't expect me to work directly with her. I try not to be in the same room with my ex-wife these days. It's my only defense to stop myself from imagining all the evil things I want to do to her."

Anna raised an eyebrow. "Your secret is safe with me."

He scowled and handed back the piece of paper. "I haven't kept my feelings about her too secret. It was the dartboard I have with her picture on it that clued in my family."

Against her common sense, Anna happily registered Caleb had very few feelings for his ex. She hated to admit it, but she was becoming so attracted to him, there were little insecurities popping up about the other women in his life. It was silly because it was obvious he still saw her as one of the mean girls from high school. He thought they were all greedy, self-absorbed, and shallow. It would take some time for him to see her as she was now if he ever did. She wasn't even sure if she'd changed enough. Sometimes even she battled her mean girl from ten years ago. Sometimes it was incredibly easy to be mean. If something wasn't going your way, you needed only to boss someone around, make them feel less about themselves, and march right over them. The only problem was you left a string of victims behind you as Wendy left Caleb behind her, and Anna vowed she wouldn't be that way.

"I really appreciate your help on this. It seems one thing after—"

"No problem." He turned to go back to the kitchen. He was all business, once again. To him their discussion was over, but it was okay because Anna needed to make a phone call to Gladys.

Chapter 15

When Caleb returned to the kitchen, he was full of conflicting emotions, and Anna was at the heart of it. At lunch he'd wanted to tell his mother what he had found out about her lost investment but kept it to himself against his better judgment. He questioned why he hadn't revealed Anna's secret. Normally, he would have confronted the situation with her full knowledge, but something made him hold back. He hated he was becoming such an easy mark, but he'd fallen for that pleading look in those beautiful eyes. It was as if he were the only one who could help her restart her life after her father's crimes. He worried it was exactly what she wanted him to feel.

"Hey, Chef," Caleb's sous chef, Mickey, stood in his path and crossed his arms across his bulky chest, revealing a food stain on his sleeve. "We finished the prep work for tonight's meal, even though *some of us* had to work through lunch." He stressed the words "some of us." The sous chef was an unhappy man.

Caleb drew in a breath and scowled. Mickey was formerly a part of Wendy's household staff, and she told him repeatedly she didn't care for the man. If Caleb remembered right, her exact words were he made her feel creepy. Caleb wondered why he'd ever let this guy come onboard in his kitchen. Life without him here would be easier, but when he and Wendy divorced, Mickey was kicked to the curb. He was an excellent sous chef, and there wasn't anyone else with as much experience. Against his better judgment, he'd hired Mickey for the club. A decision he often regretted.

"I'm sorry Mickey. I certainly thought you could handle a little prep work on your own. Why don't you take a break?"

Mickey's chest puffed up. "I can handle anything. It's one thing to have confidence in somebody and it's another to dump the grunt work on them." Mickey turned quickly and picked up one of the many checklists Caleb kept around the kitchen for prep and clean up.

"If you don't enjoy working here, you're more than welcome to find somewhere else. I hear the donut shop is hiring."

Mickey hung the clipboard back on a nail. "What a wonderful idea, but this club pays better than any other place in town. Besides, you couldn't manage around here without me, especially with the amount of time you spend *out* of the kitchen." He gave Caleb a sideways look. It was true, Caleb had been spending more time out of the kitchen with Anna working at the country club, but it wasn't any business of Mickey's.

"Were you this difficult to work with when you worked in my ex-wife's house?"

"There wasn't much to complain about because it was a better-run kitchen. The stupidest thing you ever did was let go of Wendy. She was class, I tell you. No wonder she took her maiden name back so fast. God forbid she be associated with the Armstrong family."

There was a look in his eyes Caleb hadn't seen before. Was it adoration? Mickey was fiercely loyal to Wendy, even if she let him go. Maybe it was a case of unrequited love? The poor kitchen boy and the rich girl? Why not? It'd worked for him. But why would he come work with her ex-husband, a man he had to despise? Caleb tried not to dwell on it, but there was always the possibility Mickey had taken the job out of revenge. It made him angry to think the sous chef had taken the job at the country club to make his life miserable. It wasn't right to think bad of people, but, as Caleb watched the sous chef wipe down a counter, he couldn't help feeling his suspicions might be correct.

Caleb turned and checked the menu list for tonight. The sauce for the chicken parmesan would need to simmer for a couple of hours. Why wasn't he smelling it? He looked around for the demi sous chef. "Curtis, where's the sauce for the chicken parm?"

Curtis sprung up off a metal stool in the back and quickly pocketed his phone. "Mickey told me it wasn't necessary to prepare it until right before it's time to serve. He said it would go bad if we did it too early."

In theory, Curtis was Mickey's assistant, but Mickey took orders from Caleb. It wasn't Mickey's job to decide how to cook the sauce.

Caleb shot a glance at Mickey. "And who's the chef in this kitchen?"

"You are, sir." Curtis stiffened, his head rising, shoulders squared.

"It's best you keep how a kitchen hierarchy works in your mind and get going with the chopping. One little thing can make us run late, and then we're in trouble with the dining room."

"Yes, sir." Curtis bounded to the walk-in cooler for ingredients.

"Time for my break." Mickey beamed a mischievous smile.

It was one more thing to deal with. Caleb said a little prayer for patience because he wasn't anywhere near the peaceful state he normally achieved when he was in the kitchen. First, Anna showed up after ten years and revealed her dad took money from his family and now he was on the edge of mutiny in his own kitchen.

Chapter 16

Before Anna had the chance to contact Gladys about getting her job back, a call came in from the prison. She had just gotten home and kicked her shoes off when her father's name lit up her cell phone. "Excellent news. I'm being released early. They don't have enough room for the violent criminals, so the prison board is granting an early release to nonviolent offenders with good behavior records."

Anna froze as her father continued with light banter on the other end of the line. This wasn't excellent news. Now she would have to deal with him along with her challenges here in Redbird Creek. He would eventually discover she no longer lived in New York, and the only hope she had was he wouldn't find out where she went.

"Isn't it wonderful?" he asked. Anna didn't respond. "I thought you'd be over the moon, but you barely sound excited. Daddy's coming home."

"Great." She tried to make it sound like she was happy for him, but she wasn't even convincing herself. "What will you do now?" Anna was almost afraid of the answer he'd give.

"I'll be living with you, of course. What else would I do? Where else do I have to go? Don't tell me you there's no room in your place for your old man? Come on now, family is family. If you have a room with an unobstructed view of the city, I'll stay there. Also, I have a list of foods I need you to stock in the refrigerator. I've been without the comforts of home for too long." He laughed to himself.

Jenny knocked on Anna's bedroom door. "I'm ordering takeout. Do you want some?"

Anna rose, opened the door, nodded, and gave her a thumbs up. Whatever she was ordering, Anna was hungry. Jenny tiptoed out.

Anna knew her father's release from prison would happen one day, but she hadn't thought it would be so soon. "When will you be released?"

"Probably on Monday. Can you pick me up? I know you'll have to take a day off work, but I'm sure there aren't too many events going on that Monday, anyway."

"Uh, about that." Anna sat up straight on the bed. She had never been good at lying to him when she was a kid, and she doubted she was much better now. She pondered whether she should tell him the truth or try to delay his arrival.

"About what? Come on, kid. It's time to spring your old man. We have to get Holman Enterprises up and running."

Her father would never ask if she was willing to get his business going. He assumed she was happily waiting in the wings to work for him. It was always like this from the time she was twelve years old when he told her to smile big at the investors. In the beginning, she thought it was exciting. Now she wanted nothing to do with it. She wouldn't let this happen. There was no way she was going to let him run her life. "I can't pick you up. Can you call Mom?"

There was a brief silence. "Why would I call her when I have you?"

Anna couldn't ignore the anger boiling inside of her because of the assumptions her father made and the entitlement he felt he owned in her life. In the past, she never said no to him. Now it was possible, and she liked the exhilaration of the freedom it promised her.

Her father would never expect her to say no to him. He didn't do well with anyone refusing him, and it was why he made such a great con man.

"I can't do it." She hoped it would put an end to it.

"Well, your highness, I had no idea your schedule was so crowded. I suppose I can get a bus ticket and you can pick me up at the bus depot. I don't know why you can't be there, but I'm coming home, and I'm going to need you again. Whatever it is you've been keeping yourself busy with needs to stop. Daddy's coming home."

"I have to go. Bye, Dad." Anna ended the call with shaking hands.

Her father was coming home and there wasn't even a home for him to come to. Tears poured down her cheeks. She opened her door to the hallway to see if Jenny was still out there. If she had heard some of the conversation, Anna wasn't ready to have to explain everything. Jenny seemed to really like her, for now, and she wanted to keep it that way. Why did Anna already have a better relationship with Jenny than she'd ever had with her own parents?

"Hey, Anna, how was your day?" Jenny came up the stairs, her face flushed. "A golden retriever escaped, but he only got a block away before I caught him. I was locking up down there. The pups have gone home, thank God. The food should be here in about ten minutes. Redbird Creek may be small, but they have great delivery. She motioned toward her open apartment door. "Come on over. We can eat in my place."

Anna swiped the tears off her face and followed Jenny into her apartment, hoping her housemate wouldn't notice. Once inside, she took a seat at her kitchen table.

"Mrs. Peterson dropped off her cat. She treats that animal like it's her baby. She put a pink tutu on him. I don't even know why I allow cats in a doggy daycare..." Jenny's earnest green eyes softened as she focused on Anna. "What's wrong with you?" She placed a hand on Anna's arm. "Was your phone call bad news? God, I'm so sorry rushing you off the phone. Here, let me give you a hug." Jenny reached out and gave Anna a little hug.

Anna relaxed and sobbed.

"Oh my gosh, this is terrible. What happened? Did somebody die? Did your dad die?"

"Hardly," Anna mumbled. "He's getting out for good behavior."

Jenny looked relieved. "Is that all?" She stopped, a realization coming into her eyes. Slowly she repeated. "Good behavior? As in someone who's in jail good behavior?"

Anna realized her mistake right after she said it. In her frustration, she let out her secret to yet another member of the Armstrong family, and she didn't even care. The burden of it all became too much, and she was a sucker for a kind word and a hug. Jenny was so easy to talk to about anything.

"I have some iced tea in the refrigerator. My mother says anything can be settled with a rocking chair and a glass of iced tea."

"That's good. You should stitch that on a sampler."

Jenny rolled her eyes. "No need to get out the needle and thread. My mother recites it often enough I've memorized it. Come on now, tell me what's going on."

As they sat there companionably, Anna told Jenny about her dad. The schemes, the cons, the trials, and the eventual jail time. To Anna's surprise, Jenny didn't judge, didn't scold, but sat and listened.

When the food arrived, they dug in and Jasper sat with his head on Jenny's foot on the off chance she might drop a stray bite. Jenny had ordered an extra-large helping of chicken lo mein, and Anna agreed there was nothing like carbohydrates to make a girl feel better.

Jenny slurped up a noodle. "Wow. I have to say out of all the housemates I've ever had, you win hands-down for being the most interesting."

"Yeah, well, I bet I would be a lot happier if I were a little more boring."

"So, you didn't really understand your father's business was to steal money from people, not invest it for them?"

"No. I spent most of my time arranging his parties and get-togethers. I never considered the business part of it. If I had, I would have gone to jail as well."

Jenny sat back and took a drink of tea. "It's a good thing you didn't know, then."

Anna debated about telling her the next part. Talking to Jenny released all the frustration she endured over so much of her life going out of control. But how would Jenny feel about her when she discovered her own mother was one of her father's victims?

"What?" Jenny asked, setting down her glass. "You look like there's something else you want to tell me."

Anna's lip trembled. "You're pretty good at reading people."

"Comes from spending my days with creatures who can't talk but want to let me know what they're feeling. I study everything about them, and it works, even if they're canines."

"So, you're a dog whisperer?"

"Not even. I'm perceptive, that's all." Jenny picked up several strings of noodles with a pair of chopsticks.

Anna wasn't sure whether she should tell Jenny about her mother. When Caleb found out, their relationship changed. It might be difficult to live in the same house with her if she became angry at the news of the swindle. Anna liked Jenny and knew if the situation were reversed, she would want to know. She had to tell her, even if it meant she would lose her friendship. "I found out the other day your mother invested one thousand dollars with my father."

"She did?"

"Yes. She forgot about it and now she wants her investment back, with earnings."

"Wow. That's a lot of money to her. What did you tell her?"

"Nothing. Caleb knows. He said I need to pay her back right away or he'll tell the country club about my father. One word and he can get me fired."

"Caleb," she smirked. "He always was a tattle tale. The mood he's been in lately, he might do it."

Anna, who was eating part of a piece of chicken, choked at hearing him described that way and laughed at Jenny. "Seriously?"

"Probably not, although he has changed since the divorce. He dwells on the negative sides of people. It's probably because Wendy's bad side got past him and now, he's bound and determined to pull it out of anyone he sees."

"He doesn't like me because of the girls I ran around with in high school."

"Oh, you mean the Queens of Nasty? Yeah, we all remember the famous group of vipers. I was younger than you, for sure, but you girls made history with some of your stunts."

The Queens of Nasty. A fitting name. Why was it after all the tricks they pulled, they never got in trouble? They were never expelled or even suspended. Nothing like having friends in high places, but was it really a good lesson for a young person to learn? Kids on the right side of town didn't get punished for bullying or even breaking the law. Looking at it from this side, the school's acceptance of their behavior was wrong. Other kids got into trouble, but never them.

"You're right, and I'm now seeing how unfair it all was. If it makes you feel any better, I'm not like that anymore, and I'm ashamed of my behavior in high school."

Jenny reached out and touched Anna's hand. "Anna, really, I know you've changed. I wouldn't have rented the room to you if I thought you were one of those plastic fingernails, fake eyelash, hair extension mob of women. You're not like them. Well, not anymore. I guess there was a decent human being inside you trying to get out. If you ask me, it was the threat of prison time that turned you around. You got scared straight. Even though what you and McKinzie and Wendy did wouldn't be considered a crime, there were still no consequences. Life with your father made you see consequences for the first time. Now that I think of it, a little prison time is what the rest of those girls need."

"Yeah, well, I wish your brother would see me for who I am. He still considers me one of them."

"Did I mention Caleb is the most pigheaded brother I have? Surprisingly a tough call when you have two knuckleheads to choose from. Don't get me wrong, Sam has his days, but Caleb is the all-time champion. Give him time. He'll come around."

"In the meantime, what am I going to do about my father?"

"I hate to say it, but you're going to have to resort to something you won't be comfortable doing."

"He's still in New York. The prison is upstate and will bus him to New York City, and he wants me to pick him up at the terminal. I can't do that."

Jenny smiled. "No, silly. Tell the truth. It's not too hard once you get started."

Chapter 17

Caleb was waiting for Anna when she walked into her office on Friday. "We have a problem."

"What now? Are you still having trouble with Mickey?" Anna's voice sounded weary.

"It's the crab claws. Half of them are spoiled. It looks like they emptied the tanks and gave us a bunch of rotten fish."

"Bad crustaceans."

Caleb didn't enjoy her clarification. "I'm a professional chef and know the difference between bad fish and crustaceans. In the future, I'd prefer it if you wouldn't correct me when it comes to the classification of food in my kitchen."

Anna gave a mock salute. "Yes, sir, *Chef* Caleb." She put extra stress on "chef" to make her point.

"Let me show you."

Anna followed Caleb's brisk walk to the kitchen.

When they set foot in the kitchen, Caleb guided her over to a container of crab claws.

She covered her nose with her hand. "Oh my God. That's awful. Can you get any more?"

"Nope." Caleb covered his face with a white dish towel.

"This can't be happening. Who did you order them from?"

"Joe at Beamer Fish. I guess I should've stayed with Alan's cousin. I take full responsibility for changing up things before a big event." He tapped on the number tacked to a bulletin board by the door.

"Have you already called to complain?"

"Alan liked to be the one to handle business with his cousin. I spoke to him, but because I changed the fish vendor, he told me to take care of it myself. I called Beamer Fish and was told they're very sorry, but they can't help me. They didn't even apologize and told me sometimes fish go bad and there's nothing they can do about it."

Anna's eyes grew big flashing green at him. "And you let them get away with it?"

Caleb looked at her incredulously. He regretted having to come to her with his problem, but according to Alan she was the one who was assigned to deal with this kind of thing. "You make it sound so easy. As you can see," he extended his arm, "I have a busy kitchen to run. Seeing as Alan won't help me out, I was hoping this fell under your job duties. You can use the phone in my office."

He led Anna to an office nook off the kitchen. When Anna sat behind the desk, it was amazing how small she looked.

She lifted her chin, looking ready for battle. There was nothing more appealing than a strong woman. "Let's see what they say to me."

"Go for it." Caleb encouraged, although he doubted she would get anywhere with the guy at Beamer Fish.

She reached across the desk littered with cookbooks and a laptop. He handed her the number written on a scrap of paper and, even though it was a simple gesture, the heat between them sizzled. He had been trying to ignore it, but her presence and the light smell of vanilla perfume was making his head spin.

She fumbled with the number as he drew closer. She scooted the chair over away from him. To Caleb, it looked like she was feeling it too.

"Do you want me to put in the number?" he asked in a deep voice.

"No, thank you." She made a second attempt at putting in the numbers and, once successful, put the phone on speakerphone and stood up.

A grizzly voice answered on the first ring. "Beamer Fish."

"This is Anna Holman from the Redbird Country Club. We need to see about getting another shipment of crab claws."

"Great. We can have some over there this afternoon."

Anna turned and looked up, bumping into Caleb's chest. She gave him a quick thumbs up and a smile.

Whether it was because he wanted to intimidate her or because he liked being near her, he wasn't going anyplace. "What about the bad batch?" he whispered.

Anna turned back. "Oh, and we have a shipment of rotten crab claws we'll need you to take back. Why don't we settle for calling this an exchange?"

"Hold up there a minute, little missy. You never said nothing about an exchange. I'm not running a charity here."

"And neither am I," Anna gave her best don't-mess-with-me tone. "We have a big wedding reception here tomorrow. If we don't have your crab claws to serve tomorrow night, you can bet I will let it be known it was Beamer Fish who dropped the ball and wouldn't do anything to make it right. These crab claws were for the Broussard wedding reception. Maybe you've heard of them? It really is quite a special occasion here in Redbird Creek. Anybody who's anybody will be there. You know we used another fish distributor the manager of the club was perfectly happy with, but we decided to give you a chance this time. As soon as I get off the phone, I'll type up an email to send out to all our club members. The same club members who use your services for their parties."

"Now wait a minute—"

"Sad when you consider it all started because you wouldn't do right by us over a batch of rotten crab claws, but a true cautionary tale of how small businesses fail."

"All right," he shouted on the other end. "I'll take back the crab claws. Who are you, anyway? I thought I'd be dealing with Alan since he's dumped his cousin. Trust me, lady, you're nothing like him. They got new blood over at the country club?"

"They sure do. I'm the event planner, Anna Holman, so you'd better get used to me. You try to cheat us, and there will be consequences."

"Great." His tone was sullen as he hung up the phone.

Anna placed the receiver on the hook and Caleb stepped back. "You'll have a fresh batch of crab claws this afternoon. Does that give you enough time?"

Caleb smiled. "It'll have to." Seeing Anna in action wasn't too different from seeing Wendy commanding a set of decorators or insisting her bridesmaids wear rhinestone hair clips on the same side. Ordering people around was something these girls did extremely well. "I've learned something about you today."

"You admire my grace under pressure?"

"You mean girls sure know how to put the screws to a man. Good to see you haven't lost your touch." The closeness between them still seared through his body. He shouldn't let this happen. She was a direct threat to him and his family and seducing him might be another tool in her arsenal.

"Some people are easier to handle once you outline what's in it for them. In this case Beamer Fish was about to lose business from the very people who can keep them in the black. Simple economics. I'm surprised you don't know that by now."

He needed to let her know he wouldn't be taken down so easily. He waggled his eyebrows and gave a little grin. "You know, it's always tight working in the kitchen. You seemed a little, I don't know, uncomfortable being so close to me. Anything you want to share?"

Anna tugged on her ear. "Excuse me? I don't know what your problem is with me. I'm doing my job the best I know how. If I've made mistakes, I'm sorry, but frankly, we have a big show to put on tomorrow, and the last thing I need is some kind of prima donna chef. If you have something to say, just say it."

Anna was out of breath with her proclamation and as she tried to leave the tiny office, she tripped over a stack of cookbooks on the floor. As she tried to get her balance, his gaze slipped to her. He stopped himself from steadying her. Being physically close would break down this act he was putting on and be a sure way for her to see through it.

"Problem? I don't have a problem, except for the fact you might look good on the outside, but you were spawned from a family of con artists. I could expose your little secret at any moment, and I should, considering my mother was your father's victim." He snapped his fingers. "That's it! I know why you're here. You're working an elaborate con for the old man. You work your way in and set up these entitled suckers for another round of pocket fleecing. Did I guess right?"

Anna stepped forward, raising her hand to land a solid slap on Caleb's face, but he caught her wrist before she made contact. He slipped his other hand around her waist and pulled her closer.

Caleb immediately regretted the coldness of his last statement, but his gaze was riveted to her full lips. What would it be like to kiss them and then kiss them again? He leaned down, intending to place his mouth on hers and kiss her with all the force of the pent-up frustration between the two. The background noises in the kitchen softened as he focused in on the breath between them. He leaned closer.

"Hmmm," a voice hissed from behind them.

Anna pulled away and saw McKinzie standing in the doorway, tapping her foot with murder in her eyes. Caleb hadn't shut the door behind him.

"Really? Flirting with the help now, Caleb? I expected better of you." McKinzie's eyes flashed.

Caleb's words were hoarse as he stepped back. "No, I'm not, and you know me better than that. You didn't say you were coming by."

"I didn't know I needed to, but I guess there was a lot going on I didn't know about."

"Don't worry about it, McKinzie," Anna assured her. "You can be sure it will never happen again."

"No, darling. *You* can be sure it will never happen again. Even though we've had somewhat of a slow start, Caleb and I are together, and the last thing we need is some social-failure event planner thinking she can ever land a man who belongs to me. You're already on thin ice around here, so watch your step, honey."

Anna's face clouded over. The confidence he'd seen as she spoke on the phone to Beamer Fish had faded away. He never should have put Anna in this situation. McKinzie was a part of their past, and it was evident from the look in Anna's eyes McKinzie's opinion still meant something to her. It was unbelievable to him he was even dating McKinzie. It was as if he saw her clearly for the first time in his life.

Caleb spoke up. "You're out of line, McKinzie."

"Yes," McKinzie smirked. "Because, according to you, I should be totally agreeable after finding my boyfriend in a clinch with a coworker?"

"McKinzie..." Anna pleaded.

McKinzie flapped her hand in the air, as if dismissing Anna like a servant. "I don't care. One word to Alan and I can make sure you're finished here."

Anna straightened her blouse and drew closer to McKinzie. "You say Caleb is lowering himself flirting with the help? Aren't you attempting to do the same thing, McKinzie? People keep telling me you're the last one to get married in your little group besides me. It's amazing how many times I've been told that. It must be embarrassing for you. Seems to me there's a little desperation in your voice. Desperate—not a good look for you."

Anna marched off, with McKinzie still glaring at her.

"So, what did you need?" Caleb asked.

McKinzie turned her attention back to Caleb. Her voice changed to an almost childlike tone. "I don't know. You haven't called."

It was obvious to Caleb that McKinzie was desperate for validation from him. "I've been busy."

McKinzie shot a look in Anna's direction. "I can see that."

"I'm sorry, but can we talk about this later?"

McKinzie snuggled up for a peck on the lips. Her action seemed so impersonal to Caleb and nothing like what he experienced with Anna. He needed to end this before she got her hopes up too high for a future they would never have.

"Why don't you come over to my place later? I can cook for you for once," she whispered.

"Thanks, but..."

McKinzie stepped away and slung her bag over her shoulder. "You're busy. Fine. I'm willing to wait."

As McKinzie strutted off, Caleb thought of the near kiss he'd shared with Anna and, for the first time in his life, something was different. Happy. Through the roof. Excited physically and emotionally. This was what all those love songs were about. Anna made him feel good. Better than good. His mother always told him when he found the right girl, he'd know it. It would be an inescapable truth. Was Anna the one? Even with the trouble she brought?

"No." He tried to shut down the warm feelings. "No. No. No. She's nothing but trouble and don't forget she's a coworker. Nothing good can come of this."

He repeated the chorus of no's a couple more times, but deep in his heart, he knew he was lying to himself.

Chapter 18

The night before the golf tournament, Anna was busy making sure the sign-in table was ready after sending Gladys home for the night. Registrations had increased, but Alan wanted to make it easy for club members who forgot to sign up ahead of time to still get in. Gladys fairly swooned when she learned she was no longer fired and swore her allegiance to Anna for the rest of her living days. Anna was greatly relieved to have the help. She and Gladys made a good team, and she couldn't have pulled off the tournament without her. The golfers would begin the next morning promptly at seven. There were more rustlings with Caleb's staff during the day, which made Anna nervous with so much at stake. Caleb was stubborn and mule-headed, but Mickey, the sous chef, kept inserting himself into situations. She hoped they'd make it through the golf tournament and wedding reception.

Anna struggled with the leg of the table, trying to lock it in place.

A man wearing expensive cologne and a stiffly pressed white shirt was suddenly next to her. "Here, let me help you with that. I excel at straightening things out. After all, I am a doctor."

"Thank you."

As she straightened up and stepped back, she realized her knight in shining armor was slightly tipsy.

After the table was set to rights, the man straightened and extended a hand. "Dr. Reese Broussard. The runaway-to-Vegas groom."

So, this was the famous Reese she'd heard about. A group of his friends had rented the club bar for the evening to have the bachelor party. Anna guessed country club boys didn't feel comfortable mixing with the commoners when it came to bawdy behavior. The sons of the upstanding and wealthy didn't cavort, and if they did it, wasn't in public. The one allowance they made was for the women sent in to entertain them.

He slid his arm around her shoulders and leaned into Anna. The straight strands of his sun-streaked dark blond hair brushed back now suddenly fell into his eyes, making him look like Brad Pitt and Matt Damon all in one. Good looking and a doctor, it was a wonder he'd lasted as long as he had in Redbird Creek. His resemblance to Caleb was striking.

"Well, hello there. I've been waiting for the female entertainment all evening. You know they told me it was something about not being able to get a stripper pole into the club. I guess with you we won't need one." He put a hand to her cheek and moved his thumb slowly over her lips.

Anna pulled away as Reese put his other hand low on her back and drew her to him. The whiskey on his breath was overwhelming. She attempted to extricate herself, but he grasped her tightly.

"Oh yes, you'll do fine." He moved in to kiss her before Anna had the chance to pull back.

He tasted like whiskey and cigars. What would Wendy think of her new groom planting a kiss on a woman he'd just met? Anna struggled and finally he released his grip on her.

Stepping back, she gulped. "I'm sorry. You have me mixed up with someone else. I'm the club event planner, not your entertainment for the evening."

As if unable to comprehend her protest, he pulled her back again. It didn't seem important to him she didn't have a choice in their romantic embrace. She might be on the club's payroll, but it didn't mean she was on his. "Event planning is only a fancy word for providing entertainment, isn't it?" He attempted to lower his lips onto hers again. She put both hands on his chest to free herself when a throat cleared from behind them.

Reese released his grasp, and Anna looked up to see Caleb standing in his white chef's uniform, arms crossed against his chest, looking disgusted.

Chapter 19

Caleb tried to hide the anger mounting inside of him. "Sorry to interrupt, but, Anna, if you can pull yourself away from the groom here, we have a problem in the kitchen."

"Of course." Anna smiled at Reese. "If you'll excuse me."

"Don't take too long, baby." He lifted her hand and placed a kiss on it. Had she been willingly kissing him? If she were part of a scheme to con people out of their money, it wouldn't be too far for her to go to do this.

As they began a fast-paced walk toward the kitchen, Caleb whispered, "How long has that been going on?" Caleb wasn't sure what he was feeling, but he didn't like what he'd seen. He knew he shouldn't be blaming her, but he was mired in confusion.

"It just happened."

"Well, I guess congratulations are in order. You certainly move fast, but I wouldn't want to be the one to tell Wendy."

"No. It's not like that. He was drunk, and he grabbed me. I was trying to get away from him."

Caleb shook his head in disagreement. "Didn't look that way to me. Must feel good to get one off on one of your old pals."

"I don't care how it looked. He kissed me because he thought I was part of the entertainment for his bachelor party. I told him I was the club event planner, but it didn't seem to faze him." Was she embarrassed he caught her trying to seduce a groom, or was it something more?

Anna let out a disgusted groan.

Caleb was a little surprised about her attitude. Surely this wasn't the first time she'd been caught doing something she shouldn't. "Was there something you wanted to say?"

"It's your attitude. Assuming things about me when you have no idea what actually is going on. Making assumptions is what my father does, and you don't want me comparing you to him." She let out a sigh. "What's the problem in the kitchen?"

"Oh, nothing. I thought I'd better end your little scene before you got yourself into trouble."

Anna gasped. "Got myself into trouble? Are you serious? The man was all over me. He thought I was part of the floor show."

"And are you?"

Anna's eyes widened and her cheeks turned a deep red. She was beautiful when she was angry. Caleb tried to block his feelings. What would it be like to kiss her right now?

"What kind of person do you think I am?"

"Hmmm. Seeing as you were on the phone earlier with a man whose aim was to rob the people of Redbird Creek…"

"That's not fair." There was a break in her voice, and Caleb realized he'd gone too far.

Even a con man's daughter had feelings, or at least she made it look like she had them. His reaction might have to do with what he'd seen. "Sorry. You're right. It wasn't fair. What did your father have to say?"

"Nothing." Her tone was dismissive. Whatever her father said, she obviously wouldn't be sharing it with Caleb. "Thanks for helping me with Reese. I'm not sure if it would be a good idea to tell Wendy about this. He was drunk. I'm sure he wouldn't do anything if he was sober."

"Sure."

Anna walked away.

Caleb had been sure he'd walked in on Anna willingly kissing Reese. From the expression on her face when he accused her, though, he now wasn't so sure. He also couldn't deny he wanted to know.

Chapter 20

The next morning Anna sat at her breakfast table staring at a box of cereal. Jenny was having a special Saturday daycare for all the townspeople going to the golf tournament and reception. She hired a couple of high school kids to help if the wandering golden retriever made a dash for it. From the sound of the happy howling below, it was a full house.

The morning sun streamed through the red gingham curtains with carefully embroidered strawberries adorning the hemline. Those strawberries were a simple thing but were part of the world of Anna's hometown. Living in New York surrounded by concrete and chrome, she never would have had as much peace as she felt here. Anna decided she would do anything to stay in Redbird Creek. This was her home, and Caleb had no right to take it from her. She wanted to stay. She thought about a for sale sign she noticed outside the old skating rink. The now-shuttered Redbird Rink bore a weathered sign showing a cardinal wearing roller skates flying around in a circle.

If she scraped off the peeling red paint and covered the exterior with a fresh coat of white, the building would look like new. For a moment, Anna let herself visualize the big open space as an event center. She imagined it a place people would rent when they needed a sizeable space for a function. Weddings, parties, craft shows—practically anything. She could make a go of a place like that, but who was she kidding? Anna didn't even have the money to pay back Caleb's mother, let alone invest in an old decrepit skating rink. She wondered how much of the kitchen was still intact.

It would be a beautiful day if Anna survived getting through the golf tournament and reception. She took a spoonful of cereal, although her stomach was a little rocky. She would do well to eat light during the day. Tonight, after the reception, she'd be hungry enough to empty the refrigerator, but even the mention of food this morning made her queasy.

She usually wasn't this nervous before an event. Anna handled the Mitchell wedding, one of the most sought-after invitations in New York state, without even the slightest worry. She was organized and detail oriented and left little to chance. Why was it today she was running a golf tournament in a small-town golf club and she was acting like the president of the United States would be attending?

Anna took a drink of coffee, letting her nose draw in the comforting smell. She thought about her objective. She needed only to focus on each part of the day. Live in the present and keep an eye out for the future. They would do the official opening then the tee off and send out golf carts full of food until lunch time.

That was when Anna realized why she was nervous.

Her unease was all about Caleb and how they'd left it last night after the incident with Reese. Her mind slipped to the time in Caleb's office when she was sure he would kiss her. Her heart was going so fast so hard she was sure she'd damage a rib. One more second and he would have kissed her. The tension between them returned. What would she say when she saw him again? "Hey, Caleb, been dreaming about you all night and remembering your arms around me, holding me close."

The thought of those words terrified Anna. What if something like that came out of her mouth? It might slip out when she least expected it, and what good would that do? If Caleb knew how she felt, he might have a wonderful laugh about how he flabbergasted her and hadn't even kissed her. What if he talked about it with all his chef friends? Did Caleb have chef friends? Guys and girls who sat around swapping recipes? Who were his friends?

As Anna slowly made her way down the stairs, Jenny rushed to the front desk and pulled a jar of dog biscuits from a shelf. "The natives are getting restless." She looked at Anna and paused. "You look dazed. Are you nervous about the golf tournament?"

Thank goodness Jenny thought she was worried about her job.

"Yep. Really nervous."

"Don't worry about it. You've got this and what you don't have, my brother will be glad to jump in and help you any way he can. He's always been a boy scout."

Anna's cheeks heated at the mention of Caleb's name.

Jenny looked closely at Anna, smiled, and tipped her head to the side. "Are you blushing?"

"Huh?" Anna pulled at the collar of her shirt. It was suddenly scratchy and a little tight. "Uh, no. It's hot in here. Don't you think so?"

"I can see you do." A wicked little smile played on Jenny's lips. "Do you have a thing for my brother?"

Anna didn't answer, knowing how vulnerable she was at this moment. She liked Jenny, but the feelings she was having for Caleb were all too new and too dangerous.

"You do!" Jenny squealed.

Anna didn't know if it was a look of pity or disgust on her housemate's face. Whatever it was, the secret Anna was having a hard time admitting to herself was now in Jenny's hands.

"Caleb and you? Well, all I have to say is..."

Anna waited. Would Jenny hold against her the fact her family had such a checkered past? Surely, she wouldn't want her brother consorting with a bunch of scam artists.

"...he finally fell for the right girl. I'm not so sure whether you got such a good deal. Did he ask you out?"

"No. Of course not."

Jenny nodded. "Oh, you're at that part. The I'm-attracted-to-you-could-you be-attracted-to-me part. Has he kissed you?"

Anna's face burned now.

"I'll take your expression as a solid yes. I'll have to congratulate him on stepping up in the world. You're tons better than sniveling McKinzie." Jenny started for the door.

"No, wait," Anna called after her. "Don't say anything. He almost kissed me, or at least maybe he was planning to kiss me." Anna let out a frustrated grumble. "I have no idea what's going on in his head. He doesn't even like me."

Jenny smiled big. "Oh, he likes you. He's liked you since high school."

"But he was Wendy's boyfriend."

"More like one of Wendy's captives. She went after him like a sale at Macy's. Once they got married, he got plenty tired of his social-climbing superficial wife. He didn't measure up to her standards, and she wasn't his kind of girl."

"What kind of girl does he like?"

Jenny grabbed a frisbee off the shelf and juggled it with the jar of dog biscuits. "One like you."

An hour later, as Anna finished speaking to the assembled crowd and the first team of golfers prepared to tee off, Gladys waved her hands, signaling Anna from the edge of the crowd.

"What?" Anna asked a little too harshly and quickly regretted it. The only thing she wanted to worry about today was the tournament. What could Gladys have to tell her that would take her off track?

"Your mother is on the phone and insists you speak to her." Anna had left her cell phone on her desk. Hopefully there weren't other calls waiting for her concerning today's event.

"Tell her I'll call her back."

"She said she'll keep calling until you talk to her."

"Good Lord. On today of all days my mother has to have a crisis?"

"Whatever it is, she sounded really worried," Gladys added.

"Fine. You stay here and make sure to answer any questions the golfers might have. I'll be back as soon as I can."

Anna rushed to her office, passing Alan on the way.

"Is something wrong?" he asked.

"Um, I needed something from my office." Anna hoped her excuse would be enough to get him farther down the hall.

"Isn't that what we pay Gladys for?" His mustache twitched.

"It's personal. You know, a woman thing."

Alan's face took on the color of beets. "Be quick about it." He clearly did not want to discuss the matter any further.

When Anna called her mother, she was out of breath. "What is it, Mother? I'm in the middle of a golf tournament."

"Yes, well, I thought you should know your father is on his way there. I thought he needed to stay in New York and report to his parole officer, but he doesn't seem to be concerned about following the conditions of his parole. I'm only glad they didn't put one of those ankle monitor things on him."

Anna felt like she'd swallowed a brick, making her regret the bowl of cereal she ate for breakfast. "Here? How did he find out I was in Redbird Creek?"

"He called and asked me what was going on with you and well, I buckled. He makes it impossible to keep a secret from him. You know me."

"Why? Why come here? There's no money to be made here. He's already worked this crowd."

"Well, he can't stay in New York now, can he? He's already cheated everyone we know here."

"This is awful. I'm already stuck covering a thousand-dollar investment he bilked out of Mrs. Armstrong. I don't have any savings to cover all the people he plans to cheat."

"So, why don't you tell the people there he was recently released from prison and not to invest any money with him? Simple."

"Simple for you. You're sitting thousands of miles away. If I tell these people he's a crook, not only will they not associate with him, but they also won't associate with me. I'll lose my job."

"And what's the problem with that? I didn't raise my daughter to work for places like the Redbird Creek Country Club. You should be in a higher station in life, my dear. This is fate happening for you, and it's a good thing. Trust your mother on this." She made it sound so simple.

"No. I like this job and don't want to lose it. I like making my money honestly and not worrying about the police knocking on the door."

"Don't be silly. You were never in any danger of that happening. It was all your father. I know you enjoyed living off the money he made for us. We lived like queens and frankly, we deserved it."

Anna sensed heat on the back of her neck. It was clear she was the only one in her family who had changed—who wanted to be a better person. "You seem to forget that unlike you I had no idea what was going on. We were living off someone else's money. The people he cheated worked hard for their savings. People like Mrs. Armstrong, who worked double shifts as a nurse caring for others. People who came home exhausted from a long day making money the honest way. When was the last time you were exhausted from a hard day's work? Can't you see the problem with what you're saying? I swear, you're as sick in the head as he is."

"Fine." Her mother's voice turned cold. "Your sick, unfeeling mother, who was trying to help her daughter, thought you'd like to know he's on his way. I guess you don't appreciate my kindnesses."

"I do. I do." Anna took a breath. "When will he be here?"

"He took back the Porsche he bought me before he was arrested and sold it, which gave him the money to book a flight to Texas. I drove him to the airport an hour ago. I give him a few hours."

Anna stared at her phone even after her mother hung up. He was on his way. If her father came to the club, he would insert himself into everything normal she struggled for in her life and ruin it. She remembered a time when she was a teenager and excited to be going out with a boy at school. Her father supported it, which was unusual for him. Normally, he wanted her to focus on his business enterprises. Anna thought he might finally be letting her live her own life. She didn't know the boy's father was a real estate tycoon and her dad was sizing him up for a con. When the boy stopped calling her, she thought she'd done something wrong. She confided in her father, but somehow, his opinion of the boy changed. He went from being a nice young man to a no-good punk. The boy's father testified at her father's trial, telling the jury he'd been lured in by Nick Holman's daughter. The way he talked about Anna made her feel dirty. Even though she was as much a victim as he was, he didn't see it that way. Neither did anyone else. It was this experience Anna reflected on every time she began to get close to a man.

Anna tried to put the thought of impending doom behind her. She had a job to do for however long she'd be able to hold onto it. She went to make sure the waiters who would drive along the golf paths offering fresh baked blueberry muffins and an assortment of coffees went out on time. For the afternoon round, the muffins would be replaced by drinks from the bar and hors d'oeuvres Caleb was preparing in the kitchen. When she stuck her head in the kitchen this morning, things didn't look like they were going well. Mickey was in a heated argument with Caleb and was holding up a clipboard filled with signatures. She backed out, not wanting to get in the middle of it. She hoped Caleb would hold his staff together through the reception tonight. Every time Mickey spoke, the other kitchen workers nodded their heads in agreement like they were his mindless minions. Anna decided the best way not to worry about what might go wrong was to concentrate on the tournament.

Chapter 21

Caleb was going over protocol with the waiters when he saw Anna headed toward the dining room, tablet in hand. Concentrating on the screen, she didn't notice a stray chair out of place and solidly knocked her ankle on it.

"Uff," she grunted as she hit the floor.

Before Caleb had the chance to get to her, McKinzie strolled up behind her. She wore a short green golf skirt and white polo top, looking like a golfing magazine cover girl. Her auburn hair was pulled back in a shiny ponytail under a ball cap.

"I hate it when I don't have my phone with me when something as delicious as this happens," McKinzie laughed.

Anna struggled to get up and McKinzie continued to laugh. "Sorry I couldn't help you ramp up your Instagram."

"You're as clumsy as you are useless." McKinzie's words were mean and uncalled for and a cruelty she had chosen to ignore, and he wasn't sure why. He set his clipboard on the table and reached over to help Anna to her feet.

He gave McKinzie a sideways look. "Don't you have a little white ball to hit across a field somewhere, McKinzie? We're all kind of busy here."

McKinzie, who had been smiling indulgently at Anna's pain, now quickly changed her facial expression to a pout. Her lips curled down as if she were a small child. "I wanted you to wish me good luck before I teed off."

"Good luck," Caleb's hand didn't leave Anna's elbow.

"That's it? Don't I even get a kiss?" She looked expectantly into his eyes and turned her cheek toward him.

Caleb didn't want to kiss McKinzie, but by now, the entire room was watching. To not kiss her would be humiliating for her.

He stepped away from Anna and kissed McKinzie on the offered cheek. "Good luck."

"That's my dutiful boy."" She praised him like she was rewarding her pet poodle. "I'm off to win the tournament while the two of you work, work, work." She raised her hand in the air as she sauntered away, not even bothering to look back at a man she supposedly loved and wanted to spend the rest of her life with.

"You all right?" Caleb directed his attention back to Anna. She looked more than all right to him, but he wasn't going to let what he was feeling escape. It was best not to lead her on as well as McKinzie. It was only smart to keep his distance from this group of vipers. One was bad enough.

"I'm fine. I knocked my ankle. I shouldn't try to look at my tablet and walk at the same time."

"That would help." He gave her a sarcastic look but couldn't stop himself from smiling as she rubbed her ankle.

They had a business relationship and even though he'd slipped once, he didn't plan to do it again. "You're going to have a long day on your feet, Anna." He eyed her heels. "There's no way I'd let one of my cooks wear shoes like that. Let me see your ankle."

Anna pulled away as he reached out for her arm. When his fingers touched her skin, she trembled.

"I'm not going to bite. I was checking to see if you're okay."

"I'm okay."

"I heard what McKinzie said. I have my issues with you, but you don't deserve to be laughed at. She can be cruel."

"Thank you. I'm feeling a little overwhelmed, I guess. How are things going in the kitchen?"

Mickey's face flashed in Caleb's mind. The sullen look his sous chef regularly sported was now on some other members of the staff. "Not well. I'm only hoping we can get through lunch."

"Don't even joke about something like that.""

"I'm not joking. This might be something even the great Anna Holman can't handle."

Anna looked worried. More worried than he had ever seen her.

"I'm sorry. I thought you were tougher than that. At least you would've been tougher in high school. Forget what I just said."

"It's not you. Well, it is a little. The kitchen situation scares me," Anna whispered.

"I'm doing the best I can. If I were smart, I'd fire Mickey, but I'm afraid others will quit if he leaves. It's a tough situation, but not worth getting upset about. Don't worry about the kitchen. I've worked in kitchens for most of my adult life, and they're always full of drama. We've got this, Anna."

Even though Caleb hoped to reassure her, a tear slipped down Anna's cheek. "My father was recently released from jail and found out I'm in Redbird Creek. He's flying here, today. Now he knows I've been avoiding him, the last thing he'll do is warn me. He'll get a ride from the airport to the country club and get here as fast as he can. What am I going to do?" More tears came and, as they did, Caleb reached out and touched her cheek.

"Don't cry. Don't they say there's no crying in event planning? Besides, what can he do? He's now an ex-con, which means he's rehabilitated, right?"

"Yeah, right. He's a thankless, manipulative, overbearing man. He views me as an employee, furthering his enterprises. Just because he's my father, my rights aren't as important as his."

Listening to Anna, Caleb suddenly felt fiercely protective. Had her father been abusive? The thought sparked anger in him. "What exactly are you saying?"

"No, nothing like that, but he always included me in all his plans and has never once asked me what I wanted to do. When I was younger, I went along, but I'm not that girl anymore. When he was arrested, I tried to make a change in my life. I've been trying to be a better person, although you may not see it. I didn't understand what he was doing, but I do now, and I won't be a part of it."

This was the most honest Anna had been with him and he hated to see her suffer. "Tell him what you just said."

"Don't you think I've tried? It's like he doesn't hear me."

"Or doesn't want to. Keep him out of your life, Anna. You know, this is where my mother would say it's time to turn out the lights and let God guide you through it."

"I like your mother."

"I like her too, although she's full of wise sayings which inspire anyone but are almost impossible to do."

Anna gave a weak smile. "You're right. I have to be strong now." She lifted her chin, and what a lovely chin it was. "Back to business. I should make sure the first round of golf is going okay, and you can deal with the kitchen staff."

Caleb's resistance to this girl, who had been nothing but trouble, was faltering. He couldn't let that happen. Still, he heard himself saying, "I know we don't get along, and I'm not sure if we ever will, but I want you to know if you need help with something, call me."

"I'll be fine."

"Sure, you will." Caleb only wished he believed her.

"Turn out the light and let God lead me through the dark. I promise I'll keep repeating that one today. I still have one good ankle, after all." Anna stepped outside to the waiting golfers.

Chapter 22

"Wendy Moorefield Broussard on line two"." Now Gladys had finished most preparations for the golf tournament, she was helping answer phones in the central office.

Anna didn't mind Alan utilizing Gladys in this way if she finished all her work because sometimes keeping Gladys occupied was easier than having her hanging around.

"She wants to discuss things about her reception tonight."

Anna picked up the phone in her office, shutting off Gladys on the intercom. "Wendy? May I offer my congratulations on your wedding? I'm not sure if I got a chance to say it before."

"You make it sound like I landed a big fish."

Didn't you? Anna thought but didn't say. "You'll be glad to know the kitchen is working furiously right now to prepare the absolute best meal for tonight's reception. You won't regret letting us do your reception."

Gladys came in, out of breath, and stood right next to Anna.

"Excuse me one minute." Anna put her hand over the phone, "What? I thought you were working the phones."

"A bunch of cooks just went out the front door. Mickey Durham convinced the kitchen staff to walk out. You should've heard what they were yelling. I ran right down here to tell you. There's no way we can serve lunch or get the dinner out tonight."

Anna's hand tightened on the phone, hoping to shield Wendy's ears from any news of mutiny.

"Mickey walked by with everybody else behind him. Boy they were mad. Something about the union and getting his grievances heard."

"I'll be there in a minute." Anna removed her hand from the mouthpiece. "You're kidding. How can I help?"

"If Caleb's there, put him on the phone."

"Sorry, he's not. What can I do for you?" Anna didn't have time for Wendy to get around to the point of her call.

Her old friend launched into a laundry list of last-minute requests ranging from seating arrangements to not placing flowers near the bride's table because of her allergies. Anna wrote it all down at a feverish pace, wondering why she was having to deal with this today instead of last week. Wendy should've called her days ago or, better yet, emailed her. Typical Wendy, never considering the impact of last-minute requests on other people.

Even though she didn't feel it, Anna put on her most cheerful voice. "Sure. No worries. We'll get right on it."

"Fine. One more thing. I would rather not see my first husband at the wedding reception I'm having with my second husband. Please make sure he stays in the kitchen at all times."

Her comment answered the nagging question in Anna's mind whether Caleb and Wendy harbored any old feelings for one another. From the sound of her request, it hadn't been a friendly divorce. After Anna hung up, she showed the list to Gladys.

"Wendy wants all this done before tonight."

Gladys gave a whistle. "Holy gob smackers! That's a long list."

"Yes, well, we'll deal with it after we figure out what's going on in the kitchen."

Chapter 23

Caleb turned as Anna came rushing through the doorway out of breath. She glanced around the empty kitchen. "Why isn't Alan here helping you with this?"

He smirked and shook his head in disgust. "For your information, Alan called me after Mickey left and informed me the kitchen was my responsibility and he still expected me to come up with two meals without a staff. I've been running from cook station to prep station trying to prepare lunch for the country club members."

"What happened? They all left?" Anna grabbed an apron off a hook. Gladys followed her lead, found another apron, and put it on.

"It was Mickey. He didn't feel like Alan paid enough attention to a demand for more wages and convinced the others to walk. I never should have hired him. I knew he was a troublemaker, but he's a talented cook and a hard worker."

"What can I do?" Anna asked.

"Yeah," Gladys repeated, with a little dreaminess in her voice, as she let her gaze roam over Caleb. "What can I do, you giant hunk of a chef?"

"Gladys." Anna gave her a look.

"Sorry." Gladys was now staring at her soft brown shoes. Caleb gave Gladys a little smile.

Their willingness to volunteer was admirable and something he would expect out of a good person, but how in the world was he going to turn these two into competent line cooks? "Anna, start buttering that bread so we can put the sandwiches on the grill. You'll find the butter in the refrigerator and use the big butter knife in the drawer."

Gladys stepped up in her apron and gave a mock salute. "What do you want me to do, boss man?"

Caleb bit his bottom lip for a moment and looked at Gladys's red cheeks. "How are your allergies today?"

"Good." Gladys sniffed and ran a hand under her nose wiggling it. "You can wash dishes."

Anna did as she was told and produced bread ready for the grill. Caleb and Anna worked side by side as if they'd been working together in a kitchen for years.

A tendril of sandy blond hair drifted down from Anna's upswept style and she pushed the strand back behind her ear. Caleb glanced over for a moment and just as quickly went back to work.

Anna was furiously buttering another piece of bread when Caleb stepped behind her. He stretched a hairnet over her head.

"I know the last thing you want to do is put all those curls up in a net, but those are the rules."

Anna reached up and touched the back of her hair. "Thanks."

Caleb bristled. "With everything else going on today, we don't need the health department showing up for a surprise inspection."

When the last plate went out, Caleb leaned against the counter and crossed his arms. "We did it. Good work ladies."

Anna rubbed her temple with her palm. "I'm going to need a nap after all that work."

Caleb laughed. "If only. Now we have to figure out how we're going to pull off dinner." He let out a tired sigh.

"I need a nap too," Gladys parroted Anna's motions almost exactly.

"Before you snuggle up anywhere, can you run back to the office and make sure there aren't any more problems we need to solve?" Anna asked Gladys. "We also need to get on Wendy's list."

Gladys let out an enormous moan, took off her apron, and trudged out the door.

Caleb rubbed the back of his neck. "People don't realize how exhausting working in a kitchen is."

"Which brings us back to us having no kitchen staff for tonight." Anna added. "I'll be here, but I'm not enough. Can we call Jenny?"

He put his hand to his chin, his eyes raised. "Not a bad idea. We can call the entire Armstrong family. My mom would be a godsend. Where do you think I learned how to cook?"

"Wonderful. You must have quite a family," Anna checked her watch. "My dad is probably driving this way right now."

"Okay. We can put him to work here too."

"My dad wouldn't be caught dead doing menial labor. When he gets here, I can't make any guarantees on my presence in the food production line."

"It's that bad?"

"My dad's presence can be...all consuming. He has a way of taking over and making everyone follow him."

"Sounds like a cult leader." Caleb unbuttoned the top button of his chef's uniform.

Anna took off her apron. "Same principle, but the religion is money."

"Other people's money, don't you mean. Like my mother's."

Anna rolled her eyes. "I'm still trying to get enough to pay her back."

"Sure, you are." The discussion of her father triggered anger in Caleb. "What you did today was, well, above and beyond what I expected, but it doesn't mean you're forgiven."

"For the sins of my father. Do you hear how unfair that is?"

"And it's fair he bilked an old lady out of a cool grand?"

Anna hung her apron on a hook. "Fine. I'll be back to help if I can."

"Don't worry. The Armstrong family will run this kitchen tonight. At least I know I can trust them to not steal the silverware."

"Great. I'm going to be busy with your ex-wife's list of demands, anyway. Which includes a request you stay in the kitchen and not make an appearance at the reception. Not everyone is taken with the great 'Chef Caleb.'" Anna drew closer to Caleb and lowered her voice. "One more thing, Caleb. I know you consider me a monster because of who I called a friend in the past. You're granted that, but I need you to know, whatever happens, I am not that girl."

"Okay." All day every time he'd drawn close, there was an electric current pulsating through him. Now, as she stood less than an inch from his chest, he experienced an unnerving sense he might lose control.

"And if you ever need a kitchen help or even someone to listen to you, I'm here. Although I don't know why."

"Gee thanks." He stepped away from her and picked up a dish towel off the counter. "Kind of like you're now friends with Gladys, the girl you used to make fun of every chance you got. If that's what you call friendship, I'll pass. I know how you girls work. You befriend someone until you get what you want. And you want me to let it slide that my mother was a victim of a Holman family scam?"

"I suppose you would see it that way, and as long as you're doing a quick analysis of me, here's something I've observed about you. Whatever it is you have going on with McKinzie looks convenient but a little stifling. If you hate our type so much, why would you become involved with her and why in the world would you marry Wendy? Are you too scared to branch out?"

He stiffened at her suggestion. "I'll admit the situation with McKinzie isn't ideal, but I can handle it. I like our relationship the way it is."

"You may judge me, but you're not all that different from me, Caleb Armstrong. You have someone in your life with their hooks in you. Tell me, do you genuinely care for McKinzie or does it feel comfortable having a woman you can call your girlfriend? Did Wendy affect you so much, now you're on to Wendy Two or possibly 'the revenge' of Wendy?"

"I'm nothing like you. McKinzie is difficult, but she's never tried to steal from my mother."

Anna whispered under her breath, her voice breaking, "And neither have I."

Caleb was prepared to say more but, seeing Anna's look', reached out and took her by the waist, pulling her into an embrace. His kiss was tentative as he pressed his lips sweetly against hers, as if tasting a fine soup. The intense feeling grew stronger. A million things went through his mind as he was swept away by the moment. Why did this feel so right when so many things were wrong? He kissed her again and lost control.

Caleb backed her to a wall as their kiss continued, searching, and finding each other, powered by the pent-up feelings they both carried.

At the sound of footsteps in the hall, Caleb pulled away as Alan approached, his eyes cast downward on a sheet of paper. It was apparent Caleb's biggest problem was getting over thirty seconds to kiss this woman. It was probably for the better.

Chapter 24

"Magnificent job getting through lunch, Caleb. I've been on the phone with the union, and it seems we can't get the negotiations going until Monday. Can you make it through tonight?"

Caleb was flushed and breathing a little too hard for a normal, unaroused person. But Alan seemed not to notice. "Sure. I'm calling in reinforcements," Caleb assured him.

Alan's focus bounced from Caleb to Anna. "You do look a little tired, you two, but you make a terrific team. I'm only glad I didn't have to throw on an apron."

Anna noticed her boss looked relieved. She realized Alan was so good at delegating, she wondered what he actually did.

"Hopefully, tonight will go as planned." Anna doubted her own words as to whether it would go smoothly after everything else.

"Fingers crossed." Alan gave a slight smile. "Anna, I need you out here to help with the afternoon brackets. There was an unfortunate incident with a golf cart on the third hole. We need to make some adjustments."

"Sure." Anna removed the hairnet and ran a hand through her hair. She turned to Alan. "Let's use my office to work on the next round of brackets, okay?"

"I don't care where we do them as long as we get them done and posted. Lead the way," Alan motioned.

Anna patted Caleb on the back. "Oh, and, splendid job, Caleb. You really had me hopping."

By the look of confusion in Caleb's eyes, Anna debated whether he thought she meant the lunch or the kiss still lingering on her lips. She wasn't sure herself.

While Anna worked with Alan readjusting the brackets, Gladys quietly came in and sat on the table next to the copy machine. She kept bouncing her knee up and down, causing the copy machine to rattle.

As they wrapped up the tournament schedule, Alan, his mustache twitching, cleared his throat, his beady eyes glaring at Gladys. "What is it, Gladys?"

"Uh, I need to speak with Anna."

Alan rose from the chair. "I'd better get back to my office."

As Alan left, Anna grabbed the new schedule as it came off the printer. "What's gone wrong now?"

"Oh, nothing bad. I really need to talk to you." She jerked her head to the door in an attempt at a nonverbal shove. "Out there."

"Whatever." Alan waved a hand as both women scurried out of her office.

"What's so important?" Anna asked once they were out of Alan's hearing.

"I got a bite."

Confusion crossed Anna's features. "I'm sorry. I'm not following. Something bit you?"

"No. I was on the God Bless You dating website, and someone sent me a virtual tissue." She leaned closer and whispered, "It's for people with serious allergies."

Anna was dealing with the imminent arrival of her father, a golf tournament/wedding reception, and conflicting feelings about Caleb. Why would Gladys imagine she had time to reflect on her love life right now? And a dating side for allergy sufferers—really?

"Great. I hope you have a wonderful evening. Don't forget your antihistamine." Anna began walking to the dining room to repost the new schedule.

"But this guy's different. He asked me about my allergies. It was like he wanted to know."

"Great."

"No, you don't understand." Gladys followed Anna and grabbed her by the arm. "Nobody wants to know about that stuff."

Anna grabbed a thumbtack off the board and attached the new schedule. The golfers waiting for the new brackets came over. Anna patiently worked her way through the crowd, trying to exit to her office.

One woman, with silver gray hair winging out at the sides of a purple golf hat, tapped on Anna's shoulder. "We'd like to lodge a formal complaint. I plainly asked if we could play through and the group in front of us..." She leaned close to Anna's ear, "Painfully slow..." She straightened up slightly. "...refused to let us play through. According to the rules, ignoring a common courtesy is grounds for elimination, isn't it?" She tilted her head slightly forward, playing the part of the wronged party.

"Who was it?" Anna asked.

"McKinzie and Mimi Carmichael. I mean, really? They act like they own this club."

It didn't surprise Anna her old friend McKinzie and her mother chose to be blatantly inconsiderate to the other players, but she couldn't very well kick them out of the tournament for it.

"Maybe they didn't hear you?"

"It was pretty obvious they did, especially when McKinzie called us old biddies."

Good old McKinzie. She insulted all ages. Anna realized Gladys was still by her side, no doubt wanting to talk about her virtual date with a nasally challenged suitor. Anna decided she would employ an Alan strategy. "Gladys, why don't you talk to McKinzie to let her know we don't appreciate her behavior on the golf course."

Gladys gulped. "Me? You want me to tell McKinzie to behave?"

Anna looked innocently at Gladys. "Sure, why not?"

"Because McKinzie is mean."

The woman in the purple hat nodded in support of Gladys.

"Um, thanks for the opportunity and all, but this is more something you should do," Gladys gulped. "You're her friend, after all."

Anna realized she was defaulting to her former self. It was easy and comfortable. The old Anna would have dumped McKinzie and her mother on Goopy Gladys without a second thought, and this selfish action was what she was about to do. It was easy and convenient and benefitted Anna, but she'd made a choice not to be that person anymore.

Her phone rang, and when she checked the screen, she saw an unfamiliar New York number. It might be anybody, but it was possible her father picked up a burner phone along the way. Her heart sank. She dismissed the call with a slide of her finger. If only all problems could be swiped away. "You're right. I'll speak to her." If stress were a tightly wrapped blanket, Anna would be in danger of suffocation right now.

Anna found McKinzie sitting at a table in the indoor dining area with her mother, downing a margarita on the rocks, ice cubes clicking against the glass.

"McKinzie," Anna took a seat at the table. "May I have a word with you?"

"What can I do for you?" McKinzie put a dab of salt on her finger from the rim of the drink.

Mimi raised her hand to signal the waiter for another.

"I've been told you were impolite to some golfers this morning. We here at Redbird Creek Country Club would like to remind you this tournament is for fun and calling someone an old biddy doesn't promote a Redbird feeling of camaraderie."

McKinzie's gaze darted across the room, landing on the woman in the purple hat. "I never said anything of the sort. I don't know what you're talking about—"

"Don't you have something more important to do?" Mimi interrupted, her hand still waving in the air for a second drink.

"It seems you're my latest job," Anna answered, "and I'd appreciate it if you would promise me you'll play nice."

McKinzie put the salt on her tongue, as if she hadn't a care in the world. "You've been misinformed and frankly, if it wasn't for my family, this golf course would be a nine-hole course with windmills and a fiberglass replica of the Eiffel Tower." McKinzie waved her hand through the air in a shooing motion.

It must be nice to be a queen.

Ten years ago, or maybe minutes ago, she was like her. Callous, cruel, and uncaring. Anna noticed Caleb in the corner having a discussion with one of the waiters. They had returned from their golf course deliveries and were lined up for their next set of trays for the following round. He looked over at McKinzie and Anna and raised one eyebrow. Anna feared she would have to deal with Caleb and McKinzie. She questioned why she stupidly chose to return to Redbird Creek. Caleb made his way over.

Chapter 25

"McKinzie." Caleb approached the table. "I've been hearing all about you and your mother on the golf course. You even shocked the waiters, which with this crew is quite a feat. Surely you can mind your manners?" He looked squarely at Mimi. "And you should be telling your daughter this."

Mimi scowled.

"Funny you should mention manners," Anna added. "McKinzie and I were discussing that very thing."

McKinzie looked from Anna to Caleb, registering a frown. "Your coworker here is full of herself. I would never insult another golfer."

Mimi piped in after a waiter set down her fresh drink. "She wouldn't. I didn't raise my daughter to behave like a bully. Surely you wouldn't take the word of the help over us. You're practically family, Caleb, dear. What is Anna to you?"

"She's nothing," McKinzie snapped before Caleb had the chance to answer.

Looking at Anna, it was obvious to Caleb that McKinzie had gone too far this time.

Anna clenched her fist in front and closed her eyes tightly. Upon opening her eyes, she spoke in low even tones. "You are a bully. You can play the righteous socialite all you like, but I know you. I grew up with you, McKinzie, and I used to be like you. I know exactly what you said and how you said it. You're rude, entitled, and, frankly, annoying. Calling someone an old biddy may not be a capital offense but denying it and acting like you're the victim in all of this is a little much, even for you."

The chatter in the room died down significantly as the most interesting gossip of the week was playing out live. McKinzie paled and stuck out her bottom lip then raised her pleading gaze. "Caleb, are you going to let her talk to me like this?"

McKinzie wanted him to come to her defense, but looking at Anna, he couldn't. This fight had been simmering between these two for days, and for once, he refused to let McKinzie have the upper hand.

He smiled. "If anyone knows you, it would be Anna. Tell the truth now. Did you insult the group behind you on the golf course?"

McKinzie's head jerked from Anna to Caleb. "You people are ridiculous. I can clearly see we'll have to move our family membership to another more suitable country club." She looked over at Mimi who, stunned at first, began nodding her head.

Mimi held her head straight as her shoulders stiffened. "Absolutely. It would be a great honor for any respectable country club to have us."

"So, you're ending your membership?" Anna asked. "What about Wendy's wedding reception tonight?"

The question amazed and delighted Caleb. Even if they did carry through on their threats, the Carmichaels wouldn't make their dramatic exit yet. The last thing they'd want to do was not be seen at an event as big as Wendy's reception. After all, they were on the top tier of the social ladder in this community.

"I'll be there out of loyalty to my beloved friend. I respect friendships and traditions, unlike other people in this room," McKinzie huffed. "Anna, I'm surprised at you. I guess the lower class has turned you into a harsh shrew of a woman."

McKinzie turned her attention to Caleb. "As for you, Caleb, you're overworked here, and I'll forgive you for your temporary lapse of judgment. I know it must be absolutely excruciating having to work with this woman." She gestured toward Anna and glanced around the room to the others listening closely.

Caleb scratched the side of his head in thought. Suddenly he slipped an arm around Anna's waist. McKinzie's eyes widened.

"Actually, it's amazing, but I finally see something clearly. And even though you think of her as not worthy of giving you instruction, I have Anna to thank for this moment of clarity. In my mind, you and I had been going along great for the past year. Our relationship was simple. You snapped your fingers, and I did whatever you asked of me. I was the perfect boyfriend for you. Honestly, it's all I imagined I deserved or was even ready for after my divorce. This may shock you, but we were never boyfriend and girlfriend, although you broadcasted it to anyone who would listen. It was companionship between old friends, nothing more. Only, you've never been much of a friend. Your forgiveness of my recent behavior might be a sacrifice for you, but don't worry, it's not needed." He stopped and looked around the room. "I hate to have to tell you this here, but remember, *you're* the one who made this a public scene. You and I are through, McKinzie."

Gladys, who'd been standing in the background, mouth open, nose slightly running, clapped and hooted. "Atta boy, Caleb."

The reaction around the room was a mixture of shock and a few smiles covered behind hands.

Caleb was glad for the warmth of Anna's touch as he turned her to walk out of the dining room, his arm still resting comfortably at her waist.

"Boy, you were definitely saving up on all the things you wanted to say to McKinzie," Anna whispered.

Caleb continued to guide her, not to the kitchen but to a dark hallway, where he took her into his arms. "I've been wanting to do this again all day." He grabbed her as if he were a starving man in front of a feast. He lowered his lips onto hers and, to his immense joy, she returned his kiss. He needed her right now and needed her touch badly. He wished they weren't in a hallway because, even though it was dark, he wished for even more privacy. His hunger was matched by hers as their kiss lingered. This was it. This was what he'd been missing from his life. It still puzzled him why he felt this way about her, especially after the theft of his mother's money, but it seemed so right. It was as if Anna was the right girl for him, whether he agreed with Him or not. He held her face in his hands, bringing her as close as humanly possible. All of Caleb's stress melted like an ice cream cone on a scorching summer day.

The sound of her phone buzzing interrupted the moment, and Anna reached for it. She glanced at the screen. "It's from Alan. After what happened in the dining room, he might be calling to fire me. I'm guessing McKinzie marched straight to his office and relayed the entire scene, making herself the victim." Anna pulled away and answered.

Caleb was able to hear Alan's voice.

"Anna." Alan sounded happy. Was something finally going right? "I have great news! Your father is in my office."

"My father's here?"

Caleb hoped, for Anna's sake, his boss was wrong.

"Isn't it wonderful?" Alan asked.

"You bet. Let me finish what I'm doing, and I'll be right there." Anna hung up the phone. "I have to go."

Caleb stepped back. It was like a switch flipped on his emotions. "Sounds like your father's here. I guess the con begins." He laughed to himself bitterly. "You almost got me. For a moment, I started to trust you. I blame myself for falling for yet another girl like Wendy." A cold shower was plummeting over the moment as it quickly faded. It had been breathtakingly beautiful, but it was over.

Chapter 26

"Well, this is a surprise." Anna was out of breath from power walking to Alan's office. It was as if she was rushing to a fire, hoping to put it out before it spread to any other part of her life.

Nick Holman looked out over gray eyebrows, his keen blue eyes observing his daughter. Even after his time in prison, he still looked like an upper-class rich man who belonged in the houses of the Hamptons on the East Coast or Bel Air on the West Coast. His salt-and-pepper hair was freshly cut, and the new lines on his face gave him an air of trustworthiness. Not that he'd grown up rich. He was the son of an alcoholic scam artist who had trained him well .

He ordered drinks but didn't drink them and was always two steps ahead of his mark. His lips were smiling, but his eyes said a different thing. He was sending a message only Anna had the ability to interpret. Her father was angry. Incredibly angry. Her dad didn't tolerate insubordination. Not from anyone, and especially not from his daughter. She was his flesh and blood, and he expected her to act accordingly.

"I can see that." Her dad's tone was even. "I tried to call, but Alan here tells me you're busy today working as his event planner. Why didn't you tell me you took a job outside of the family?"

Anna bit her lip. "You were head over heels busy with your current job, and I didn't want to complicate things. You always taught me to be self-reliant."

"That I did." He gave a thin smile. "I guess I raised you right. You'll be excited to hear I've got a few deals going right now and couldn't wait to tell you there's a spot for you in our little family business."

"Oh, dear." Alan was oblivious to what the conversation between the father and daughter was really about. He was still glowing in the essence of Nick Holman and trusting everything was legit. Why wouldn't it be?

Anna was used to it. It happened a lot around her father. He had the rare talent to be able to sell anything to anybody at any time. It was his gift.

"We find your daughter very helpful here at Redbird Creek Country Club," Alan assured him.

"Of course, you do. I share the same sentiment." Nick winked at Alan as if they shared the same secret weapon in forging ahead with their successful enterprises.

Alan smiled back, enjoying the brotherhood with Nick.

"I couldn't run my operation without her."

Alan's eyebrows knitted together for a moment. "May I ask why you two aren't working together presently?"

Nick brushed him off. "I was working somewhere Anna shouldn't go."

"Oh, the Middle East? Perhaps working with an oil baron who thought women should be under a veil?"

"Something like that." Nick didn't correct him.

"Well, I hope you'll let her finish out this assignment, Mr. Holman. She's an invaluable part of the team today."

"I'm sure she is. It was one of the things I always loved about the Redbird Country Club. It's a well-run operation."

Alan was eating up the praises, but Nick's words sounded hollow. There was no such thing as a gracious Nick Holman. He was manipulative and hyper focused on his own end goal. If he was thanking a person for something, it meant he was receiving much more than his victim thought they had given. Sadly, they never figured it out until he was long gone.

"Wait a minute." Anna raised a hand.

These two men talked as if she wasn't even in the room, deciding her fate like she was a child.

"It's great to see you, Father, and I appreciate your very generous offer. But I'm happy working here."

Alan beamed at her words.

"And I plan to stay."

Nick came over and took Anna's hand." Exactly what I love about you, my dear." His grip tightened so much she wondered if she'd have a bruise tomorrow. "You're so incredibly loyal." His cold blue gaze gave her a look of admiration with an underlayer of ice. "I raised you right, but I'm sure Alan here realizes you're a Holman first and have obligations. He must know how torn you are, but don't worry. Family first, right?"

"Dad, I don't—" Anna pleaded.

"It's settled," he interrupted her.

Anna knew he wouldn't allow her to refuse again.

"Now you go on back to work for this fine gentleman." He gave her a pat on the butt like she was a nine-year-old.

Anna opened her mouth to speak, but Alan "offered her father a cigar. She was dismissed.

Fury blinded Anna as she ran down the hall. She was crying as she turned the corner and unexpectedly ran into Caleb's mother, Beth.

She put a hand on Anna's shoulder. "Slow down, girl. Whatever it is, I'm sure you don't have to run over an old lady to solve it."

Anna wiped a tear from her cheek. She didn't want to be around Caleb's mother. The last thing she needed was a reminder of one of her father's past victims. "I'm so sorry. I didn't see you."

"That was obvious. You were too busy letting whatever has you riled up get under your skin."

Beth directed her over to a pair of overstuffed chairs in the hallway. "Come on. Sit down. Sometimes confiding in a stranger does a world of good. No judgment, just an ear. I'm an excellent listener, or so I've been told."

Anna did as she was told. She wanted to get away, but suddenly the kindness in the older woman's eyes halted her flight. "You're here to help Caleb tonight, aren't you?"

"Sure am. I only hope I can stand letting my son be the boss in the kitchen. One tends to get pretty territorial about these things, you know. Still, we love him and are so proud of him and his job."

Anna smiled. Caleb was lucky to have a mother like this. How could her father have scammed this woman? Did he feel anything as he grabbed the cash from this sweet lady and mother of three? Probably not.

"So, what is it that has you all upset, my dear?"

"My father. He's here."

Beth lifted her head slowly. "Oh. I need to talk to him about my investment."

A rush of anxiety flew through Anna. Why did she feel so guilty when she didn't perpetrate the crime? Still, when she looked into Caleb's mother's eyes, she felt at fault. She needed to make this right.

"I've been trying my best to work out paying you back your investment."

"I'm almost afraid to say this, but I was hoping there would be a bit of profit," Beth admitted. "Your father told me my thousand dollars would double in only a few years."

A fresh rush of guilt jolted Anna, like black ink over her soul as she tried to figure out what to say next. "Here's the thing. My father might have stretched the truth a bit and, for that, I'm sorry. Truthfully, I doubt he ever invested your money." Anna took a breath. Was she crazy letting one of her father's patsies know he'd cheated them? There was something about this woman that made her want to tell the truth. The truth about everything.

Beth's eyes widened. "You mean he took my money and never invested it? But he told me about all those companies and how they were so successful. He promised me. I don't understand."

Anna wasn't sure if she should trust Beth. Sure, she seemed nice, but nice people had been known to go to the police when confronted with crime. Would doing the right thing cause Anna to lose her job and send her father back to prison? The old Anna would have stopped talking at this point to save herself, but she wasn't her anymore. "My father is here because he was recently released from jail in New York for conning people out of their money. It was much the same thing he did to you."

"I see." She let out a breath. Beth's mouth thinned and her shoulders slumped.

Anna wished her father could see this. This was the damage he caused in people's lives. He probably spent Beth's thousand dollars without even thinking about it. Even worse, he might've spent it on Anna. The thought of it made her feel even more ashamed.

"I didn't know about it until they arrested him. He never told me his business associates were really a pool of unsuspecting marks he was using to finance our lifestyle. You were probably one of his first victims."

"Your father is a handsome fellow. He was so kind to me, and I might be an old married lady, but I certainly know when I'm being flirted with. I probably made it so easy it gave him the confidence to cheat anybody."

"Don't say that. My father is a master of manipulation. He can sell ice to an Eskimo, as they say. I want you to know, I'll pay you back every penny out of the money I'm making here at Redbird Creek Country Club..." It occurred to Anna she wouldn't have the money to offer if she was forced to quit after tonight's reception. The tears returned.

"Oh, darlin', please don't cry." Beth put a comforting arm around her. "Shoot, it's only money."

It was such a kind thing to say and Anna's tears came in even stronger.

"Come on now. I'm not going to call the sheriff on you. Even though I was a bad judge of your father's character, it's obvious you had as little knowledge of this as I did. Push this away. You'll feel better."

Anna patted Beth's hand. "Thank you. I'm really trying to be a better person. I thought I had it all figured out here. I was starting my life again, but now my father says I have to quit here after the reception and go back to work for him."

Beth tilted her head to the side and pursed her lips. Anna had trouble deciphering if she was wary or concerned at this statement.

Finally, Beth asked, "He does, does he? Who gives him the right to tell you to quit your job?"

"The great Nick Holman does. He always does this to me. When he went away to prison, I was relieved. It gave me a chance to live my life on my own, but surprise, he's back and he tells me it's all over. I have to go back to being his glorified assistant, event planner. I dread the thought of it, but you know already how hard it is to say no to this man."

"Got me there, but still, don't let him take over. Fight this. He might be strong, but from listening to Caleb talk about you, you're stronger than you think."

One sentence stuck out in Anna's mind. It might be a negative thing, but she hoped it was something else. "Caleb talked about me?"

Beth's gaze softened. "Sure. If I didn't know better, my son has a little crush on you. Frankly, after seeing McKinzie skulk around, you're a vast improvement, even with your con man father fresh out of jail."

"Thanks, but I don't know what to do. Caleb was angry when he found out my father cheated you."

"I'm sure he was."

"And, according to him, I was in on it."

"You weren't, and he has to have figured it out. If it hasn't gotten through that thick skull of his, I'll make sure he gets the message."

Anna released her grasp on Beth. "Caleb is very lucky to have you as a mother."

"And I'm lucky to have him as a son. We were blessed with two boys and one girl. Every day, no matter how much they get under my skin,

I'm thankful they're around. Every day. I didn't grow up in a home like I live in today. My parents were, well, cold. I never remember hearing I love you from either of them. I decided when I had a family of my own it would be a place of love."

What a contrast Beth was to Anna's father. She had a similar beginning of sorts but broke the pattern. Anna wondered if her father ever considered having any sense of gratitude for her or if he only saw her as his unpaid employee who owed him something?

After leaving Beth, Anna felt different. Empowered. As if there might be a way to head off her father's interference. She needed to figure out how. Anna heard her father's voice echoing throughout the halls as he greeted his old friends and future suckers. He hadn't cheated too many people here, or he wouldn't be so comfortable playing the role as the conquering hero.

She desperately wanted to prevent him from victimizing these people. She had to stop him from ruining the life she was finally creating for herself. Putting on her most too-busy-to-talk walk, she made her way across the lobby, intending to escape to her office. It was at that moment she saw her father engaged in conversation with Mimi. McKinzie, probably embarrassed about Caleb breaking up with her in front of other club members, was no longer sitting at the table. Her father was skillfully portraying the oh-so-interested-in-everything-you're-saying expression he used often, and Mimi appeared to eat it up. Anna was close enough to hear it all and swallowed down a mix of anger and revulsion at the way her father was lying to this woman.

Mimi folded her hands under her chin and smiled. "So, you say your business in New York is so successful you've carved out some time to visit your daughter? Well, it sounds wonderful. Exactly what kind of business are you in?"

It was all he needed. He was truly "in" now. From there he'd flatter, cajole, tease, and gently coax Mimi out of her life savings. It was his gift and Anna's curse. Anna didn't like Mimi or her daughter, but she would never wish her father's tricks on anyone. Change of plan. Anna rushed to the table where her father was busy setting a trap.

"Miss Mimi? I hope my father isn't bragging about his so-called business dealings again. Daddy, did you tell her about the bankruptcy? It might be a good idea."

Mimi's eyes widened. "Bankruptcy? I thought you said your business was booming."

His eyes flashed dark and in an instant he took on a smooth air of confidence. "Oh, that's my Anna. She's such a kidder. If I didn't love her so much, I'd be angry right now. Of course, I've never undergone a bankruptcy. I worry endlessly about the trust and loyalty my wonderful clients have always given to me. Their money," he touched his heart, "is like my money."

I'll say, Anna thought.

"And because of the tremendous responsibility, I tend to fret over every penny. I've told her, and this is embarrassing, one day, when the stock went down one percent for about an hour, it was as shameful as a bankruptcy for me. Luckily, with my shrewd investing, it doubled in the next hour. I guess my reaction was a bit dramatic, but I guess I'm wired that way. You can understand, can't you?"

Mimi gave a slow, appreciative nod. It was like she was seeing a natural wonder in front of her. With a revered tone, she whispered, "Of course I can, Nick." She purred in such an intimate fashion, Anna was embarrassed for her. "You're exactly the kind of person I'd want to look out after my investments. I don't know if you noticed, but I'm not a young woman anymore."

"You aren't?" His tone of utter surprise made Anna's stomach lurch.

Mimi gave him an indulgent smile. "Oh, Nick, you're a cad." She giggled, heaving her large bosom.

Clearly Mimi was delighted by the attention of such a handsome man. It was part of his charm. He treated every client like he wanted to marry her, or him. The sex of the mark didn't matter to her father, the skilled con artist. Mimi's cheeks radiated into a flush, as Nick's flirting took full effect.

He looked to his daughter. "I'm sure you have work to do for the reception tonight." He stood and took Anna's elbow. "Thanks for checking on me." He tightened his grip, making Anna wince. "I love you too." Like a trained actor, he kissed her on the cheek as any loving father would.

Anna had crossed a line she'd pay for later. You never, never interfered with a deal in the works. She'd done it once before on her fourteenth birthday when she reminded him, in front of a client, they were going to miss her birthday party. He was kind and solicitous in the moment but later ordered her mother to return all her gifts. Never, ever interfere with a deal in the works. It was his cardinal rule, and violators would always pay.

Chapter 27

That night, while Wendy and Reese celebrated in the banquet room, the entire Armstrong clan bustled around in the kitchen. Jenny came a little early and got to see Anna's new office and Caleb noticed how close his sister and Anna had become. Sam, although working hard at his assigned duties, appeared to be in a talkative mood. The kitchen was becoming as comfortable as the Armstrong family home. A much nicer atmosphere than it had been when Mickey was shooting him belligerent stares. Caleb was thankful for an evening with his family, even it was slightly stressful.

"The guys can't wait for my turn as cook at the firehouse," Sam bragged to the others.

"The only reason they're watching the calendar, Sam, is because they want to get a chance to order ahead so they don't have to eat what you're cooking," Caleb shot back in the playfulness of brothers.

"Don't listen to him, Anna. I give them variety. Caleb won't even try my recipe for Spamarole. It'll make your mouth water just seeing it. Besides, you can only eat so much chili."

"Spamarole?" Anna asked.

"Spam casserole." Sam pinched his fingers together and kissed them, making a loud smacking sound with his lips.

Caleb's father, Cyrus, pursed his lips in concentration as he peeled potatoes, his thick hands making their way around them with a paring knife. He looked up and smiled at his boys. "I've eaten it. It was different, I'll say that."

With Caleb directing and his mother making sure the others stayed on task, the crew worked smoothly preparing and plating the meal for the reception. Everyone worked well together and, even though they weren't specifically trained for the jobs they were doing, they pushed through. In the peacefulness of the kitchen Anna looked more comfortable than he'd seen her.

Anna went back and forth as she oversaw both the banquet room and the dinner service. Over the clank of the dishes, Anna raised her voice to make an announcement in the kitchen once the meal was served. "Wendy wanted to let you know the dinner was great, and she wants you to serve dessert after they make their toasts at the bride's table."

"No problem." Sam slung a dish towel over his shoulder. "I'm sure the new Mrs. Broussard wants time to celebrate her latest catch, but in this kitchen, we're celebrating too. My little brother, Caleb, is now officially free of Wendy the witch, for she is now forever somebody else's problem."

"Here, here." His father raised his hand to hit a high five with his wife of many years.

"Thank God," Jenny added. "I couldn't stand that girl. Sorry, Caleb, but your taste in women hasn't exactly been stellar."

Caleb, who was busy grading chocolate into fine little slivers, smiled. "And you have so much experience in the world of dating, little sis."

"He's got you there, Jenny jelly beans." There was a gleam in Sam's eyes.

Jenny crossed her arms and stamped a foot. "Don't call me that. Not fair. I'm the youngest one, and the only girl. I don't have to be all worldly."

"Amen and thank you," Beth agreed.

Caleb's dad agreed with his mom. "You tell them, Jenny girl."

There was a buzz in the next room and Anna listened at the door. The crowd was quieting down.

"I'm going out there," she said. "Now remember, Caleb. Wendy doesn't want to lay eyes on you tonight. You're the invisible kitchen help. The speeches are starting. I'll be back to give you the cue."

As soon as Anna left, Caleb stopped what he was doing and made his way over to the porthole-sized window facing the dining room.

"I thought she advised you to stay back here," his dad reminded him.

"Did she?" Caleb's gaze never left Anna in the next room.

"Why, Caleb? Are you interested in the crowd or the little lady who just left your kitchen?" Sam asked with a hint of sarcasm.

"None of your business."

"Oooh, Caleb has a crush. Caleb has a crush," Sam sang in a voice that would be the pride of the fourth grade.

Chapter 28

Anna slipped out quietly to the dining room, where Wendy's father was at the microphone. "Welcome, everyone. Before we get started on the celebration of my daughter's wedding..."

Latest wedding. Anna searched the room for her father and found him sitting at a table with the Carmichaels. If there were any doubt he was about to close a deal, this would quash it. He had the ability to worm his way in anywhere and obviously was wiggling into Mimi Carmichael's good graces. Anyone else looking at them would think they were old friends, but Anna saw the big bad wolf preying on Little Red Riding Hood's grandmother.

"We need to settle up our golf tournament today," Wendy's father continued. He had a deep golfer's tan and snow-white hair,—the classic look of a pampered life. "When my daughter told me she agreed to let the golf tournament take place on the day of her reception, I was ecstatic." He turned to the country club manager. "Alan?"

Alan was standing in the background, along with Gladys, who was trying to balance an enormous trophy taking up over fifty percent of her height. Anna stifled a giggle thinking how awkward Gladys looked. She stopped herself and remembered she was trying to be a better person. A real friend would go over and help her hold the trophy instead of laughing at her.

Anna's boss moved forward to polite applause. He was holding a piece of paper Anna thoughtfully supplied to him earlier with the day's scores and the winning team. "Yes, and thank you. It was a wonderful day today, and we are so pleased we can share in the celebration of Wendy and Reese's nuptials. Not only that, but it delights us some of our former members came back, including Nick Holman all the way from New York City."

Even though nobody asked him to, Anna's father stood as if the whole room were applauding for him. He now wore a more formal suit and tie and, putting his hand on his trim waist, took a slight bow. One thing about her father was he always looked classy. Several women in the room beamed electric smiles as if George Clooney were honoring them with a visit. He might look a little like George, but it was as far as the similarities went. He wasn't gracious or rich, and he wasn't who they thought he was.

"Thanks." Nick waved to all four corners of the room.

Alan continued. "Yes. First, we were blessed with Anna coming back to us, and now we're delighted to have him taking time away from his successful business dealings to pay us a visit. Now, let's get down to the business of finding out who today's winner is." Behind Alan, Anna had stowed several prizes and a large cardboard check for the winner.

As Anna made her way to Alan, passing the kitchen door, she found Caleb standing next to it.

"You're supposed to stay in the kitchen," Anna whispered.

"I'm lying low. How close are we to the dessert? I see your father made it into town."

"Yes."

"He's quite the guy. I'm sure he'll have a pocket full of 'investments' before the night is over. Too bad Alan didn't tell them about that blessing," he whispered.

Caleb didn't trust her father, and by extension he didn't trust Anna. It made her feel a hopelessness inside she tried to ignore as she made her way to the front.

As she stepped forward, he muttered, "Like old times, right?"

She turned and glared at him. Was she crazy in hoping after his speech to McKinzie and the kiss they'd shared in the hall they'd declared a truce for the evening? How could he assume she was in on some scheme her father was working? He'd kissed her and made her feel so good. She started dreaming of the future. It was something she'd dared not do before. He was only too happy to remind her Anna

Holman was a mean girl, a member of a confidence scam team and not worthy of him or this town.

Anna watched her father as Alan presented the awards. She realized Caleb's about-face linked directly back to him. She had to stop this—she needed a plan. Her father was excellent at strategizing in the moment. Whatever came about, her father pulled out a slick word or phrase to handle it. It was what made him such a good con man. If he faced rejection, he found another way into someone's desires, and he wasn't afraid to zero in on something his mark felt strongly about. Anna decided to try to visit each person he spoke with and try to squelch whatever seed he might have planted. She planned to say her father would want them to conservatively consider whatever amount he advised investing. Once she got their attention, she would urge them to start with a smaller investment, perhaps only ten percent of whatever he recommended. Her father would feel it wasn't worth the effort and move on to his next victim. She was sure he wouldn't waste his time on ten percent of his target.

Caleb's last statement still stung. Her father was targeting victims and assumed she was in on the con. Being around Caleb's family made Anna realize how valuable a stable support group was to a person. Caleb had everything, and he didn't know it. Caleb was stubborn and mule-headed and deep down inside, she wished he'd kiss her again.

Once the awards were given, Anna glanced over at the Carmichael table. Anna's father chatted up Mimi and McKinzie's father, A. J. He was a robust older man with blond hair going gray and a barrel chest. Anna decided the Carmichaels would be her first attempt at a turnaround. She pulled a chair up to their table, wedging herself between A. J. and Mimi.

"Hi, Dad. Enjoying your evening?"

"Why wouldn't I be when I'm in the company of two such beautiful women?"

Mimi was glowing. The excitement in her voice betrayed her. "Your father has been telling us all about his business and some brilliant investments we can get in on from the ground floor. Isn't it exciting?"

A. J. spoke up. "Yes, this has been a very fortuitous meeting. We're always looking for ways to stretch our investments."

"Well, I've always said God puts you next to the person you need to help." Nick gave an award-winning performance of heartfelt expression.

Anna feared it was too late if both McKinzie's parents were buying her father's schtick. "I see. Well, with any investment, caution is the key." She gave a friendly smile.

"Exactly!" Nick pointed a finger at her.

There it was. His split-second ability to turn a conversation. It looked like he was telling her how right she was, but Anna squirmed. He used the same gesture whenever scolding her for doing something wrong. She knew what it really meant.

Anna went on, "Yes, I would say whatever he tells you about, it would be wise to invest a little money to start. Like ten percent of what you planned on using. You might do this only for the very beginning, you understand, until you can see if it will truly yield a profit. You shared this strategy already, didn't you, Daddy?"

Nick smiled and nodded. "Clever, my dear, but you know better than anybody how much I care about my clients. I would never suggest they take on too big a risk. The amounts I'm setting out for them are still in the safe zone but enough to see a significant return. My Anna here was always the one with the caring heart. That's what I love about her." There was an edge to his voice. In the background, Alan was announcing the winners, as sporadic applause went on around them.

"Significant returns are important, but significant losses can be devastating. Not everyone has money to burn like you do, Dad." Anna's voice held an edge of her own.

"Oh hush, Anna." McKinzie, who had been sitting quietly, finally butted in. "You don't understand your father's business."

Nick's gaze pivoted from Anna to McKinzie and finally to her parents. "You've raised quite an intelligent woman. I'm sure you're proud of her."

"Yes, it's hard for us to understand why she's still single," A. J. added.

McKinzie turned to her father. "Daddy, the last thing I'd do is listen to the opinion of an employee of the club. She's not a financial planner. She's an event planner. Now if you need her to set a table or something, she's perfect. Right?" She gave Anna a cold look. "Don't you have some trash cans to empty or something?"

"Sorry to interrupt." Anna pushed her chair away from the table. Trying to steer people away from large losses would be harder than she thought and after what McKinzie said, Anna wasn't sure if she even wanted to rescue the Carmichaels.

As Anna stood, McKinzie's face revealed a little smile. The smile of a victor.

Anna's father's expression was quite different. He was angry. His eyelids were pinched together as he tracked her movements like a hunter to its kill. He was furious.

Chapter 29

Caleb, who was busy in the kitchen, made time to return to his spot in the doorway. At one such occasion he was surprised when Wendy motioned for him to come over to the bride's table. Anna was talking to a guest elsewhere in the dining room, so even though it was against her orders, he decided to slip out. It didn't take long for Anna to spot him and there was an unsaid warning in her eyes.

Wendy placed her hands on the shoulders of a woman Caleb didn't recognize. "I realize I said I didn't want to see you tonight, but I wanted you to meet my cousin Fiona. She's visiting here before she takes a tour abroad."

Fiona glittered from head to foot, and, from the looks of her, Fiona wasn't planning to backpack across Europe, staying in hostels. This was a room service girl if he'd ever seen one.

"Nice to meet you, Fiona." Caleb gave her a brisk smile but, seeing Anna approaching, reached out and took Fiona's hand and kissed it. "You never know who you might meet at a wedding, that's what I always say."

"Absolutely." Fiona gave a come-hither smile.

"I would love to get together later to continue this conversation." Caleb's gaze shifted to Anna. "For right now, it looks like I need to get back to work, right, boss?" His comment was directed at Anna. Excusing himself, he pulled Anna away from the bride's table and pointed at her father, who was busy telling a story to the Carmichaels. "I see you and your father have wasted no time going after McKinzie's parents. I really thought you might wait until at least after the golf tournament, but what is it they say? No crime like the present." He shook his head in disgust.

"Not that it's any of your business, but I've been trying to stop him, not help him. Caleb, sometimes it seems like you see me as frozen in time. I don't steal people's money."

"Listen, as far as I'm concerned, you are a clear case of heredity and environment heaped together in one big childhood. Face it. You've been raised for this. You can be the sheep or the shearer, and the Holmans will always be holding the clippers."

Something in Anna's eyes hardened. "Fine. If that's the way you insist on thinking of me. Sure, it's tough to look a gift horse in the mouth," Anna retaliated.

At least she was finally admitting it, he thought.

"Dad was always a hard worker." Her glance strayed to the now-empty plates at the tables. "You can start the waiters on the dessert."

"You bet, boss, but not until I do one thing." Caleb slapped the white towel on his shoulder and strode to the table where her father was busy spinning his words of security and false investment.

Each table member looked up when he approached. McKinzie's bottom lip formed a thin line, the pain of their earlier split-up obvious in her eyes.

"Good evening." Caleb gave a slight bow.

To anyone else at the banquet, it looked like the chef was checking to see if the meals were satisfactory. The Carmichaels might have spawned McKinzie, but they didn't deserve to be worked over by Nick Holman.

"Even though I'm not your favorite guy right now, I thought you might like to know Anna's father here only recently came back from a stint in—"

Before he had the chance to finish his sentence, Nick Holman interrupted. "Real estate school." He shook his head boyishly in mock embarrassment. "I had a desire to become better educated. I should have done this years ago, but I guess you're never too old to learn something new, especially when it benefits my clients. Yes, it's true. I'm now qualified to advise on real estate investments as well, which is good, because I have my eye on a prime piece of commercial real estate right here in town—"

Before Nick could continue, Anna's voice came through the microphone. "I hope you saved some room because our incredible Chef Caleb has come up with a dessert guaranteed to make you want seconds. Our esteemed chef has worked tirelessly on this magnificent meal, so can we have a big hand for Chef Caleb?"

Caleb put on a perfunctory smile and raised a hand to thank the room for clapping.

"Caleb, come up front here. We have a little something special for you," Anna continued.

He shot a quick glance at Nick and marched to the front.

Anna thrust a navy-blue bag with a gold ribbon tied at the top on him.

Caleb was wary as he untied the ribbon. He pulled out a denim apron with a cupcake embroidered on it. Underneath it was stitched, "There's always time for a cupcake with an old friend." The exact words he'd said to her when they met again for the first time. For a moment, he softened. His gaze met Anna's. The cupcake represented their shared history both when they were in school and when he offered her the cupcake on the first day at her new job. It was heartfelt and sentimental and a blatant attempt to smooth over things between them. She must have also been hoping he'd cease his attack on her father until she was able to handle the situation. That wasn't happening. Caleb straightened up and reverted to his former mood as if a cold steel barrier were coming down over them.

He gave a tight-lipped smile. "Thank you very much."

"Thank you for the wonderful meals you and your staff have provided throughout the tournament and this evening." Anna glanced toward the kitchen where Jenny and Beth stood watching. "I don't know what we would have done without the fine work you and your staff did to make our evening come out so well. Let's give the kitchen a round of applause."

Polite applause went up around the room.

Alan stepped up to the microphone and put an arm around Anna.

"And I would like to thank Anna. She's a recent hire, and I'm sad to say we might lose her now her father is back in town and needs her assistance with his business. She was a valuable part of this team, and we couldn't have done it without her. Let's all give a big hand for Anna."

The crowd clapped but Anna's gaze rested on Caleb, making him uncomfortable. There were so many conflicting emotions going through him. He wanted to out her and her father in front of all these people, but it would be a terrible thing to do to Wendy and her new husband. She might be his ex, but, even with their history, he wouldn't willingly destroy this occasion for her. His desire to make things right would have to wait, and his desire for Anna, also illogical, would have to be controlled.

Chapter 30

When the last guest left, Anna was in her office making a final report for the day even though exhaustion pounded through her entire body. The tournament had been profitable, even with Wendy's discounted dinner.

Gladys trudged in with her shoulders slumped forward. She pushed back a strand of stringy brown hair as she picked up her bag. "We're all squared away. These dogs are tired." She pointed to her feet. "I'm going home."

"Great work today." Anna put her own tired feet up on the desk.

"I heard you're leaving. I guess I'll be considered for your job now. A month ago, I would have jumped at the chance. Now, I'm not so sure."

Anna sat up slightly and shook her head. It infuriated her everyone easily accepted a decision she never made. They were all going on the word of her father and Alan, not bothering to ask her what her plans were. "I'm not leaving, Gladys. Not if I can help it. Although, after a day like today...You don't want this job?"

"I thought I did, but now I understand there's a lot more to the job than I realized. I thought you made a list and threw a party. Being around you, I'm learning how to do it, but if I ever had to tackle a double event like you just did, I'm not sure if I have the brains, the organization, and even the gumption to do it, you know?"

"Well, don't worry, because I'm not leaving."

"But Alan said—"

"He was wrong. My father told him I was quitting. Alan never asked me if it was *my* plan. He assumed it was decided before I even got there."

Gladys blinked rapidly as she took in this information. "You mean your father decided where you should work? That can't be right. Are you sure? He seems like such a nice guy."

"Yes, he does, doesn't he? Don't let him fool you. If I wanted to work for my dad, I would have stayed in New York."

"It's really weird how he came down here for you. I figured you must be a valuable part of his business. You certainly proved yourself here. I wish I could be that useful. Hey, what about your aunt Janet? Who's taking care of her?"

"Aunt Janet." Anna stopped for a moment and took in a deep breath. Time to account for a lie. Anna treasured her new friendship with Gladys and it was time to treat her like a friend. "There is no Aunt Janet."

Gladys gulped. "She died? I'm so sorry. When did it happen?" She stepped forward and, putting her scrawny arms around Anna, gave her a tight hug. "I'm here for you, whatever you need. Would you like to come over to the double wide for dinner after church on Sunday? My mom makes up a mean batch of fried chicken."

"No," Anna stuttered. "I don't know how to tell you this..."

"It's okay. Let it all out. I read an article about scream therapy on the internet. Want to try it out?" Gladys let out a yelp so loud that if anyone were left at the club Anna was sure they would come running to Gladys's rescue.

"No. Please stop. Aunt Janet didn't die. She never lived. She wasn't real. I made her up."

Gladys stepped back. "You made Aunt Janet up? Why?"

"Because—well—it's complicated."

"Telling the truth should never be complicated. It's simple really. The only one stopping you from making it right is you."

Wise words from a person Anna used to harass. She was seeing Gladys in a fresh light. She wasn't a hopeless oaf. Gladys was wise with empathy only someone who had been on the receiving end of daily harassment would have. She could have been a bitter woman out to get revenge on her tormentors. Instead, Gladys didn't let them get to her, and lived her own life to the fullest, no matter what kind of abuse she received. Anna noticed Gladys hadn't sniffed since she'd been in the office. She realized those dark patches under her eyes gave Gladys character. It had to be difficult living every day with such severe allergies and yet Anna and her friends mocked her for it. Anna felt a deep shame for her past behavior and was grateful for the realization a person's perception of another could change.

"You're right." Anna slapped her hands on her thighs in agreement. "You're so right. It's time I told you the truth." Anna took her feet down from the desk and straightened up.

Gladys pulled her arms across her chest and pulled down her chin. "I'm listening."

Anna told Gladys the entire story, from her father's Ponzi scheme in New York, to prison time, to her escape to Redbird Creek. At the end of everything, it was as if she freed herself from a tangle of guilt and shame.

"So, you were a professional con woman? Tell me, did you rub the side of your nose like they did in the movie *The Sting*? I've always wanted to do that." Gladys whistled through her teeth in amazement.

"No. Sorry. I didn't con anybody. I didn't know what my father was doing until the very end. No matter how hard I try, I can't get people to understand I didn't have a clue as to what he was doing in all those meetings."

A deep voice Anna couldn't seem to keep out of her dreams spoke from the doorway. "Stop conning people. That would help." It was Caleb.

"How long have you been standing there?" Anna sat up ramrod straight. "I'm surprised you're still here. Didn't you have a late-night date with Wendy's cousin or something?"

"I do, but I wanted to let you know the kitchen is locked up tight and we're leaving."

"Great. Have a good evening. I'm sure she'll want to hear about all your recipes."

Caleb gave a quick smile.

There was a quiet in the room after Caleb left. Even though her dogs were tired, Gladys quietly stood and once again gave Anna a hug. "It will be all right. I promise. You're not a con artist. You have too big a heart to steal from anyone."

Chapter 31

Caleb woke the next morning feeling like he had eaten a big bowl of sawdust during the night. He rose and went to the kitchen for a glass of water.

Once he finished drinking, he realized he had more than a dry throat. He had a sore one. He stifled a cough and there was pressure in his chest. Great. A head cold with congestion. Exactly what he needed on his day off. The phone on his bedside table rang, and he ran back to the bedroom to get it.

"I wanted to remind you Sunday dinner is at two," his mother said. "Would you mind whipping up a dessert?"

Before Caleb had the chance to answer, he sneezed into the phone with an ear-deafening honk. "Sorry, Mom. I'm going to have to pass today. I'm sick."

"Oh boy. Normally I'd feel bad for you, but we were all elbow to elbow with you last night. Good thing I'm taking my vitamin regimen. Did you get a flu shot like I told you to?"

"I did. I got a flu shot and made sure my entire staff got flu shots. You'll probably be fine. We were all either washing hands or wearing plastic gloves. Plus, I make it a point of keeping all the counters clean."

"I hope you're right. You go back to bed and we'll come by later with a plate of supper for you. Need anything?"

"I'm fine," he said gruffly. "Thanks, Mom."

As he hung up, he experienced something he was getting used to. Anger. Something inside him rolled around unresolved, and it seemed like he was going nowhere fast. Wendy's cousin Fiona was beautiful, looked hot in the dress she wore to the reception, and, as she put it, was between meaningful relationships at the present. She was the kind of girl he always dated, or at least the kind who dated him. Sometimes he felt like a stop on the way to their Mr. Right—the guy in a higher income bracket who would make a good showing at the club or office.

Life is easier when you have excellent looks, but there was another side to it. A side people don't talk about.

People wanted to be around him, but he didn't want to be around some of them. Caleb was pleasantly surprised when in high school the "it" girls wanted him to be a part of their group. Wendy snapped him up quickly. Now he had moved on to McKinzie, who was still single and not much different. He realized he had been ignoring her selfish, manipulative, and cruel way of going through life.

These were not the qualities he was looking for in a girlfriend.

He hoped Anna wouldn't be like them, but it was turning out she was. As much as he experienced a new sense of excitement being around her, once the initial infatuation was over, she would turn out to be like all the rest of them, but with one added pressure. He had to work with her, at least until she got caught running off with someone else's money. Anna Holman was bad news all around. He should stick to his type—like Wendy's cousin. He crawled back into bed and decided to worry about it later.

Chapter 32

On Sunday morning when Anna awoke, she was thirsty and hot and achy all over. Her back hurt, her feet hurt, her shoulders hurt. Sitting up on the edge of the bed, she felt the room spin. Pushing her immune system to the very limit yesterday had caused it to take a header.

Downstairs Jasper was barking, and Jenny yelled down the stairs. "I'm coming, I'm coming, you needy Basset Hound."

It sounded like she was scolding him, but there was love in Jenny's voice. She loved Jasper more than chocolate.

A sneeze snuck up on Anna as Jenny passed her door.

"Wow. That was a big one." She knocked. "Can I come in?"

Anna went to the door and opened it.

Jenny looked more closely at her housemate. "Your face is flushed." She put a hand to Anna's head. "You're running a fever. Get back into bed, I'll bring you some juice and vitamin C."

"No, I'm fine. Really."

"Isn't today your day off? You certainly deserve it after all you've done. Rest. I got this. Let me check and see what cold medicines I have in the cabinet. Sit tight."

Anna crawled back under the blankets, suddenly freezing. The dog's barking grew to a fevered pitch. It sounded like more than Jasper. She guessed Jenny had taken in a couple of extras over the weekend. When Anna shut her eyes, the thoughts of yesterday crept in.

Her father was back in town and she feared he would soon knock at the door demanding she return to New York with him. She'd fought to control her life and decisions, but now he'd shown up to snatch it away from her. Anna glanced at the clock. Her father was a notorious early riser, and if she knew him the way she thought she did, he'd arranged an early tee time with McKinzie's parents. He was probably out on the golf course spinning his lies about penny stocks and no-fail investments. It was his way of life when they lived in Redbird Creek.

No one took notice when he went from selling cars to selling insurance to selling stocks. They would have seen it as the natural course of upward mobility. Each step of the ladder made him appear more successful and more trustworthy to the naive residents of the town. It was amazing how being a silver-haired smooth-talker opened doors and shut eyes. Her father was a master at telling someone what they wanted to hear.

"Here's your juice. I don't have any cold medicine, so I'll have to go out and get some. You don't have any do you?"

"No, but you don't have to do this."

"Sure, I do. I checked in at my mom's house and amazingly, Caleb's sick too."

Anna didn't quite know what to feel. On the one hand she was sorry he was sick but on the other, he deserved it for being so mean to her. Caleb had turned into another man in her life who felt entitled to define her. To him she was a criminal stealing old ladies' pensions and nothing more. Her thoughts drifted to Gladys as she remembered her words. Telling the truth is simple. One and done. She needed to do this.

"Too bad. Can I get Caleb's number from you?"

Jenny's head jerked slightly. "You want to call my brother? Seriously? From what I saw last night, it didn't look like you two were playing well together."

"Yeah, well, he's sick too, and misery loves company."

"I guess. Give me your phone." Jenny quickly punched in Caleb's number. "If you're sure you'll be okay, I'll run to the store. I'm leaving my doorbell camera monitor. If anyone comes to the door, you can speak into this little camera, okay?"

"What about the dogs?"

"They'll be fine. Jasper is beyond happy about having a sleepover." Jenny gave Anna a gentle smile. "Enjoy chatting with my big brother. Don't let him pick on you." Jenny began to leave but stopped herself at the door. "I know things have been bad for you with your ex-con father showing up out of nowhere and things look pretty hopeless. I'm surprised you turned out as well as you did. It's like you never had a real father to teach you right from wrong or to even tell you that he loved you."

Jenny's observation was accurate. She'd grown up with a showman, not a parent. "Thanks for saying that."

Jenny gave her a warm smile and a wink as she left. After downing the entire glass of orange juice, Anna dialed Caleb.

"Who's this?" he answered, his voice sounding uneven.

"Anna."

"What do you want?" It appeared manners were optional when Caleb was sick.

"I want to tell you something." She stopped for another sneeze.

"You sick?"

"Yes, but it's not why I called. I need to ask you to do something."

"It will have to wait until Monday. I'm not going into work today."

"As talented as you are, I don't need any cupcakes baked. I need you to listen to me."

"Fine. I'm listening."

"Okay," she coughed. "I want you to see me for who I am. Not Anna the con, but Anna, a coworker. I don't cheat people and don't appreciate you thinking I do. I've been affiliated with some shady dealings in the past, but I wasn't aware of it at the time. My father is a master con man who fooled even his own family."

"Uh-huh. You said that before. Is your strategy to say it enough times until I begin to fall for your line? I know how you work. You plan to wear me down until I finally agree with you in order to get you to stop?"

Frustration filled Anna. She was telling the truth, but he wasn't willing to listen. "Caleb. Listen to me. I need you to trust me. I'm not going to be working with my father. If anything, I want to stay and work at the country club with you."

Neither of them spoke. In the context of a sales pitch, Anna's father always told her once the opportunity was presented to the potential buyer, the next person who spoke lost.

Anna tried to wait, but her impatience overtook her. "Well?"

"I'll consider it."

"That's all I ask." The doorbell rang downstairs. Anna glanced at the doorbell camera. It was her father.

"I have to go. My dad is at the door."

"Is he now? And now we're back where we started. Happy conniving."

"Caleb, please –" A sneeze escaped in the middle of her sentence.

"Not only did you give me your cold, but now I have to accept your line of bull? Not happening."

"Yeah, well, you probably caught your cold from Wendy's cousin."

"Nope. Anything as bad as this had to come from you."

She clicked off the call and made her way down the stairs, holding a tissue to her nose and a blanket around her shoulders. She was tempted to ignore him, but there was a car in the driveway, and he wouldn't give up until someone answered the door.

"Hello, Father."

"You look terrible. What did you do?" No sympathy but there was the ever-present blame. This was her real father.

"I didn't do anything. I caught a cold."

"Well, too bad because I need your help. I'm close to getting McKinzie's parents to invest, but I need you to get Mimi on board. She seems to trust you. I guess you've got a little of the old Holman charm. Good to hear you picked up something after all my years of training. At least now you understand what my business is really about, and, the more you understand, the more valuable you are. No more lying or covering the truth, right? We know what we are. Get dressed and we'll take the Carmichaels out to brunch. Oh, and put some makeup on. Can't have them thinking you're at death's door."

It was as if the earth beneath her was caving in and sucking her down into her father's pit of evil. Did he seriously want her to go out and work a con with him? In the old days he would have said it was a business deal he needed help to close, but now he didn't even try to hide what he was doing.

She said a little prayer and, in her firmest, yet somewhat scratchy voice, said, "I can't."

"You can and you will." Her gave her a steely look. "We don't have time for this." He took her by the elbow and guided her to the stairs. "Is your room upstairs? Get a move on, girly. I'll give you ten minutes."

Anna pulled her arm away, suddenly finding new strength. "I said I can't. I'm sick."

He shook his head in disgust. "You don't look so bad to me. You always were a drama queen."

"You told me I look awful. Now you're lying to get what you want, but I guess it's all you know how to do."

Nick pulled Anna around to face him, his voice a low, angry rumble. "Listen up. I've let your behavior pass, but that time is over. You enjoyed your little vacation from reality, and you can thank me for saving you from yourself later. You will get dressed and you will come with me. Do you understand?"

Anna attempted to pull away, but Nick squeezed her arm. "I can't be a part of this anymore. I refuse to be a part of it. What's to stop me from calling the police on you?"

He lowered his eyelids slightly, as if putting down a winning hand of cards. "Because I've done nothing wrong. Come now, enjoying myself at the country club is not a crime."

Anna moved closer to her father's face and, in an even tone surprising even her, demanded, "Leave me alone. Let me live my life. I am not your employee. I'm barely your daughter."

Nick turned away, crossed his arms, and gazed out the window next to the front door of the Barkington Palace. "Fine. I applaud your independence. I should've known any daughter I raised would want to run her own show, eventually. It's the way we are, superior to most people around us. It's about time you grew up. I guess it finally had to happen, but it doesn't mean you can't help me one more time. All I need you to do is sit there and be nice to the old bag. I'll take it from there. When they agree, you're officially out. You can be a little event planner at the country club. Of course, I'll always wonder if you might not actually be in your father's business. Fertile ground." He smiled.

"My answer is still no. I don't need your permission to live my life. You act like I have to give you notice."

"I'll make you a deal. Do this, and I'll leave Redbird Creek. I'll get out of your life forever." He waited for her answer. The next person who spoke would lose.

There was the chill rushing through her body. If she tried to play along one more time, it would finally rid her of him. It was a tantalizing proposal. After it was over, she would pull McKinzie aside and explain her dad was attempting to steal from her parents. If she did reveal this truth, there was always the chance McKinzie might try to get her fired simply because she was related to him. No. She would have to let it happen and hope for the best. She would have to let the Carmichaels be her father's next victim. It was wrong, but it was a way to the freedom she so desperately wanted.

Anna wanted her freedom from him more than anything. "Fine. This is the last time, though."

With his best car salesman smile, he reached out and squeezed her arm. This time it was a friendly squeeze, but things could change on a dime. "Fabulous. Get fixed up. Glad to have you back on the team. I have to head over there now to warm them up. Don't take too long."

As Anna trudged up the stairs, a heaviness descended upon her. She was doing this terrible thing to an old friend's parents. She was back on the team. Caleb had been right all along. Jenny's words echoed in her head. She had never known a real father.

Anna met her father and the Carmichaels at the Cardinal Café, seated at a lovely booth by the window. Several bird feeders hung from the branches of a majestic oak tree out front, providing a picturesque view from the booth. Redbird Creek, Texas was famous for its cardinal population and the cafe made themselves an excellent spot to view the colorful birds. The outside of the building was cardinal red and inside red checked curtains and tablecloths highlighted the many cardinal pictures and sculptures scattered around the dining room.

Her father's head was bent close as he spoke to McKinzie. Anna sat down in an empty seat next to her father. Mimi looked casual chic in a lilac jacket and skirt, while her husband sported a gray polo and navy pants. They looked like any well-to-do couple in Redbird Creek on a Sunday morning and Anna wondered if they would dress this well after her father stole all their money.

Mimi smiled when she saw Anna. "I was hoping you would be here."

"Wouldn't miss it," Anna said.

"What can I say?" Nick feigned embarrassment. "I don't make a move without my beautiful daughter." He aimed his comment to Mimi who, from her adoring gaze, seemed to eat it up. She placed a hand over her heart as if to show how far gone she was.

After giving her order to the waitress, Anna sat back and listened as her father launched into his spiel. Mimi and A. J. listened closely. Nick was drawing them in like a patient fisherman with an expertly made fly. It was interesting how he pulled in each one of them. To Mimi, he was an honorable man. To A. J., he was a man who could be his friend. A best buddy.

"So." Nick dabbed at the corner of his mouth with a napkin after finishing two fried eggs. "What do you think?"

"It sounds like a grand investment. Where do I sign?" A. J. answered quickly. It was almost as if he didn't want to give her father a chance to change his mind when in reality the situation was turned around, but he didn't know that.

"Now, let's be conservative," Mimi cautioned. "We are comfortable with our finances, so let's not take any gambles."

Good for her, Anna thought. Nick's gaze zeroed in on Anna. This was why he insisted she join them. This was her moment to sway Mimi. A moment she dreaded. Anna fought her instinct to get up and walk away, but this was the only way she would get her father out of the picture for good. It was her ticket to freedom from him and all his schemes and cons.

"My dad seems to have plenty of takers." At least it was partly true. He had plenty of suckers to be more exact, but it was simply a sin of omission, not an outright falsehood.

Mimi kept her fingers on the table, all the while looking at Anna. "So, we might miss out on something. I hate it when everyone else in the club gets a tip which results in them making scads of money and we miss it. Well, if you say so. Go ahead, A. J. Let's do this."

That was it. The deal was sealed. Her father would make a tidy profit, and the turning of her stomach was now joining in with all the aches and pains of her cold. A sneeze came out unexpectedly, and she rose to get a tissue from a box by the register. When she was a foot away from a red floral tissue box, she noticed a man standing with his back to her receiving a white paper bag.

Chapter 33

"Here's your chicken soup, Caleb. Sure, hope you feel better soon." The man at the counter wore a white apron with "Redbird Rudy" stitched on it.

"Thanks." Caleb's voice sounded more like Gladys this morning, with nasal overtones bouncing through his words. He turned as Anna approached.

"So, the brilliant chef has to go out and buy chicken soup?" She stifled a sneeze.

He gave her a tissue. "Funny what happens when you swap a little spit."

Anna blushed.

Caleb glanced around the room. "Are you here for lunch?"

Anna gestured back to the table. "My father insisted. I'd rather be at home in bed."

An instant picture of Anna in bed crashed into Caleb's thoughts. He quickly discarded it and glanced over in the direction she had come from. His expression hardened. "Working on a Sunday? You are ambitious."

"Not my deal. He made me."

"I hate to say this but, if you keep protesting you're not in on it and yet overtly show you are in on it, it's getting hard to trust you. Don't take me for one of your marks, Anna. The fact you're here proves what I suspected all along. You're in league with the devil."

Anna grabbed a second tissue and blew her nose. She nodded. "Sure. Whatever."

Caleb, grabbing his bag, whispered to Anna. "Redbird Creek is my town and there is no way I'm going to let you get your grubby hands on these people's money." He wasn't at a wedding reception any longer. He strode to the booth where her father was working the con. The Carmichaels would not be Nick Holman's next victim.

Anna placed her hand over her mouth as Caleb spoke louder than most of the people in the cafe.

"Mr. and Mrs. Carmichael, are you aware your esteemed financial advisor and friend here recently spent time in prison for masterminding a Ponzi scheme?"

Mimi's mouth dropped open. A. J. choked on his hash browns.

"No." Caleb tilted his head to the side and pursed his lips. "I get it I'm not your favorite person right now, especially after breaking up with your daughter, but not even shallow, social-climbing people like you deserve to be cheated out of your life savings."

A. J. turned to Nick, his eyes widening and a line of color coming to his cheeks. "Is this true? You served time for a Ponzi scheme?"

Nick pressed his lips together hard, as if trying to hold in the actual truth. "Of course not. If I'd been in prison, wouldn't I tell you? This man is obviously delirious. Who is he? The cook from the country club?" He turned to Caleb. "Move on and mind your own business before I call the police."

"On what charges? Outing a con man? I've got news for you. I heard about your checkered past from your daughter." Caleb reached back and pulled Anna by the arm, propelling her in front of him. "She didn't want you to come here, and I have my own theories on her reasons. Our dear Anna, the beautiful, professional event planner, has been trying to keep you a secret because it would ruin the family business."

Anna pulled her arm away. "Stop it, Caleb. You have to know I'm not a willing part of this, but—" Her gaze went to her father, a tear forming in her eye. "What he's saying about my dad is true. My father is fresh from prison. I came here to get away from what he did. I wanted to start my life outside of his. That's all. I came to Redbird Creek because it felt like home. This is going to sound corny, but I needed this place. Maybe I was being foolish, but I hoped this town needed me."

A. J. stood and threw his napkin on the table. "Well, Redbird Creek doesn't need the likes of you or your father." He touched his wife's shoulder. "Come, Mimi. Thanks to Caleb, here, we dodged a bullet." He faced Nick. "I never liked you, Holman. You don't belong with our kind."

McKinzie scrambled for her purse and, upon standing, thrust her nose upward, but Caleb didn't miss her smile. She looked happy he had outed Anna's entire family. How long would it be before she tried to get him back?

Anna moved to the table to retrieve her bag as Caleb followed her.

Her father rose slowly from the table. "You've got a lot of nerve." Nick gave a hard look to Caleb.

"Yeah, well, one thing I can't stand is a phony and you, sir, are a first-class, lights-in-the-sky, neon-glowing example. Move on to some other town to find your victims. Redbird Creek is on to you."

"Go get 'em, Caleb," yelled one of the diners.

Caleb turned to the crowd and raised his hands. "You're all a witness."

Several heads nodded.

He turned and whispered in Anna's ear. "Too bad you're a part of this. I was starting to like you. At least I won't be one of your victims."

Anna reached up and slapped Caleb, landing a solid blow. "Congratulations. You took down my dad, but you also single-handedly bulldozed my life. I hope you feel happy with yourself when you dream about me in the middle of the night." She drew closer and whispered, "And you will." Her voice returned to a normal level. "My greatest hope is someday you'll realize I was a victim of my father, not a co-conspirator."

Caleb grunted, about to say something, and suddenly stopped.

"Shall we go?" Nick offered Anna his arm.

"I'm not going anywhere with you. You promised if I went along, you'd leave me alone."

"Did I?" He looked surprised and laughed. "Hardly."

Anna stopped cold. Even though Caleb was sure she was in on the con all along, this time she looked surprised. It was obvious, no matter what she did or said, she wouldn't be allowed to live her own life. Her father's sense of entitlement over her was clear in his eyes.

"Leave me alone." Her shoulders slumped. "I beg of you. Go somewhere I'll never have to deal with you and your schemes again. I'm a grown woman, and I deserve to live my own life."

"Your life is and will always be with me. You're a Holman."

Caleb took a stance behind Anna. He could feel her shoulders trembling. "You heard her, bub. Move on and leave her alone."

Nick threw his eyebrows together with a look of amazement. "Who are you to tell me what I can and cannot do with my daughter? I'm her father and you're nothing but a lousy cook. I suggest you mind your own business, or I'll have Alan fire you."

Nick gripped Anna's arm, but Caleb stepped forward and pushed the older man back with a solid thump on the shoulder.

"Leave her alone."

Nick, regaining his footing, scowled. "Unhand her. She's going with me."

Another gentleman, with a tractor insignia logo on his ballcap, set his fork down and stepped over next to Caleb. "He said to let her go, man. I suggest you get going."

Nick muttered, "This isn't over."

Nick left the diner, and Anna turned back to Caleb.

"Thank you," she nodded to the man in the ballcap. She turned her attention to Caleb. "I don't understand why you did that."

"Neither do I." To his surprise, as angry as he was at her, he had this insane desire to protect her. "Trust me. I only wanted to see the two of you leave town on separate buses."

Chapter 34

After the scene at the cafe, Anna returned to Jenny's and crawled into bed in her rented room. She had been so excited about coming to Redbird Creek, restarting her life. Now it was only a matter of time until Alan let her go, and, with what recently happened, no one in town would hire her. Why should they when she was caught scheming with her jailbird father to take the town's money? It took everything in her to pull up stakes in New York and come down here, but now she would have to find a reserve of energy to do it all over again. The chills were coming back accompanied by a throbbing headache. She not only found a job she was loving, but she found a person who seemed so right to be around. Caleb was a good person with an enormous heart, a loving family, and when she looked at him, she felt like she was home. Not a home she ever lived in, but the home she could easily move into. Anna had dated men for months who never made her feel the things she did after being with Caleb for ten minutes. The kisses they shared filled her in a different way. Deeper. They meant something to her. It was at that moment it hit her like a freight train. She was in love with Caleb. None of her father's illusions even came close to offering what she had with Caleb. He was the genuine thing.

Yet, with one announcement to the world, he not only halted her do-over here in Redbird Creek—her home—but any chance they would have had to be together. If there was any way to reverse time and start over with him, she would.

Jenny knocked softly on the door. "You all right? I brought you some juice."

Anna gave a soft smile as Jenny entered and handed her the juice. She reflected the same eyes as Caleb.

"No, but thank you." A tear ran down her cheek and dropped into her glass of orange juice.

"Come on now." Jenny sat on the bed and put an arm around Anna. "Tell me."

"Alan is about to fire me. I guess this means I'll be moving out, too."

"I heard all about it. My self-righteous brother had to do his big reveal in the diner, so news spread all over town. Mom called me."

Anna broke into sobs, and Jenny held on tighter. "It's going to be okay. So, what if you're part of a gypsy con family? Some of us in this town are happy to look past your checkered history."

"But the entire town is now sure I'm out to rob them. No one will ever trust me again, not to plan an event, not to do anything. I couldn't get a job at the Dollar Store at this point, even with Gladys's recommendation."

This time Jenny didn't answer, only hugged her, reaching up and pushing a strand of Anna's hair back. "You rest, okay? Take a nap. Everything looks better after a nap in the middle of the day. I'll bring you over some soup later."

Jenny returned to the doorway.

Anna extended a hand in Jenny's direction. "Thank you."

"What for?"

"Being my friend."

"You make it easy to do."

Chapter 35

Meanwhile, Caleb sat in the bedroom of his townhouse running through the speech he made in front of his friends and neighbors at the Cardinal Cafe. There was still an anger stirring in him thinking about Nick Holman shaking down his mother and the people of Redbird Creek. He grabbed a tissue and stifled a sneeze. His bulldog Emile, put his head on the side of the bed.

"I'm okay, boy." He looked into the dog's earnest brown eyes. "I'm a little under the weather. Don't worry. I won't miss any of your feeding times, but it might be a few days before we take a run in the park."

The dog panted at the mention of the park.

"Be patient. I'm out of sorts right now."

Out of sorts didn't even come close to describing what he was feeling. He was angry, but it felt like more than the potential crime he stopped. He'd lost something. For the first time in his life, he met a woman who fit. Anna understood what it was to work for a living and not depend on a trust fund. She was a girl who met challenges head on and reworked solutions, not unlike working in a busy kitchen on a Friday night when the meat for the main dish ran out. He liked that about Anna. She had the ability to handle a crisis and come out smelling like a rose. He also liked the way she smelled, the way she moved, the feel of her soft body against his. Caleb grunted, making the dog's ears perk up.

"I've got it bad, Emile. Real bad. I've switched from the purebreds and now I like someone who isn't exactly pure." He glanced at Fiona's number, still scribbled on a napkin on his bedside table. This kind of dating relationship would always be there if it was what he wanted. But was it really?

How different were the Fionas of this world from Anna? Fiona was the girl who went to parties, galas, whatever it was the well-to-do did for fun. For once he wished for a girlfriend who wanted to go to a football game and enjoy a beer and a dog. A girl who would buy paint with him to work on his house. A girl who would rub his shoulders after a long day's work and tell him she loved him. A girl he would want to have a baby with someday. He wanted that girl. Anna was what he'd been waiting for his entire life.

No, she's a criminal. She would come into his life, break his heart, and leave. Conned out of love instead of money. He needed to forget about Anna. It was better that way. Who needed to take a girl to a football game, anyway?

Chapter 36

Two days later Anna was ready to re-emerge from her room at Jenny's. She needed to clear things out at the country club. Her father hadn't bothered her, but she wasn't getting her hopes up. Typically, he waited for her to cool down and approached her when her defenses had softened. He was waiting it out, yet another sales tactic.

While sitting in her comfortable room at Jenny's, Anna made plans. After Caleb's announcement at the cafe, she couldn't stay here. She needed to start fresh again and in such a way her father wouldn't have a clue where she went. Other towns near Redbird Creek were probably as nice, but if she didn't go far enough away, there was always a chance someone here would know someone there. No. She needed to move back to a large city. There was still a possibility he would find her through her mother.

As Anna folded her wardrobe into the three bags she brought with her, she tried not to dwell on what she was leaving behind. For right now she would pick up her paycheck and hit the road. It was silly to imagine she could ever have the sense of comfort everyone else in the world easily achieved living in a town like this. It was reinforced when she related the entire story to her mother over the phone.

Lillian's answer was short and immediate. "It really is for the better, dear. You need to get away from those people. I always felt like I was suffocating when I lived there with your father." Lillian assumed Anna would be the same. She wasn't. She never had been.

When Anna stepped inside the country club, Gladys was hard at work behind a new computer in their tiny, shared office.

"So, did you get my job?"

Gladys snorted. "No. He's looking for someone else I can assist. Always a bridesmaid." She returned to her screen and typed something.

"What are you working on?"

Gladys looked up, her eyes large and an unmistakable fidget in her seat. "Uh, nothing."

Anna sidled around her desk. A picture of a moderately attractive man wearing a doctor's coat smiled back at her on the screen.

What is this?" Anna asked.

"It's the God Bless You dating site. It's happened. I found Mr. Right."

Anna cocked her head back and reexamined the screen. "Is this the guy you were talking about?"

"He's a doctor."

"Or so he says. Anyone can get a doctor's coat and put it on for a selfie."

"No. You're wrong about this. He's an allergist, and I told you he sent me a virtual tissue. He says I'm interesting."

Great. Even Gladys, with her continual congestion, had the ability to attract a man. Anna was happy for Gladys, but inside it rained down on her like another cold shower aggravating her misery.

"Well, actually he said I'm an interesting case."

"Huh? That's how he tries to interest you in a date?"

"He wants to get together for an appointment."

Anna considered Gladys her friend, and she didn't want to see her set up for disappointment. "Seriously? Are you telling me he's on this dating site so he can troll for new patients?"

Gladys's whole body drooped over the computer. "I didn't think of it like that." She looked up, readjusted her glasses, and sniffed. "So, he only wants to see me as a patient?"

Seeing Gladys's expression, Anna wanted to kick herself. Just because her entire world was hopeless, it didn't mean she needed to make Gladys feel the same. "Guess what? I'll let you in on a little secret. Sometimes I don't know what I'm talking about. You should meet him."

Gladys perked up. "Really? You're not trying to be nice or setting me up for something?"

"Really. I only want you to be careful, but you deserve to have true love."

Gladys got up from her chair and hugged Anna so tightly it almost made her cry. "I'm so excited. He lives about forty miles from here. This is the first time I have interested a man for my allergies, not driven him away with them."

Anna nodded raising her eyebrows. "Who can comprehend what magic awaits?"

"Yeah, who can comprehend the magic?" Gladys imitated Anna's tone.

"Make sure you take your cell phone and promise you'll be careful."

Gladys nodded. "You bet, Boss." She stopped on the last word as she realized her mistake. Anna was no longer Gladys's boss.

"Well, I'd better go get my check from Alan."

"Sure." Gladys's bottom lip was trembling. "For what it's worth, this was the first job I've ever worked at I really loved. I'm not sure if it will be the same without you."

Anna touched Gladys's hand. "And I'm sorry. This is the first time I experienced the pleasure of meeting the real Gladys. May I say it was an honor working with you."

Gladys smiled. It wasn't the fake smiles Anna witnessed around the club. "Don't be sorry. You're a good person, Anna Holman. I've known it all along. You can't help it your dad came into town and ruined everything."

"Actually, I'm sorry I never knew the real Gladys when I was in high school. I never should have listened to that pack of hyenas I called friends. I think we might have been actual friends."

Gladys beamed and gulped. "We can still be friends."

"I'd like to be friends'." Anna felt deep in her heart Gladys was put there to help her, even though she didn't recognize it at first. For that she was thankful.

When Anna arrived at Alan's office, he was going through a stack of paper. When she looked closer, she saw the word "resume" printed at the top of one. He was already looking for his next event planner. "Anna, thank you for coming by, but I could have mailed your check to you."

"Yes, but I'm not sure where I'm going. It's better if I can get the money now, anyway. I'm going to have to make it stretch."

"Yes. I suppose you're right. You Holmans certainly do whip in and out, don't you?"

"Not by choice."

Alan pursed his lips together, making his caterpillar mustache form a straight-line. "I hear your father's gone."

"He is?" Even though he hadn't been in contact with her, she assumed he was still around waiting for her to change her mind and join forces with him. "When did he leave?"

Alan leaned back and rubbed the side of his neck. "From what I can tell, it was Sunday night."

"Do you have any idea where he went?"

"No." There was a definite edge to his voice. "And it's a pity because the police work better if they have an actual address to track down."

Alan's mention of the police made Anna startle. "Police?"

"Your father convinced me to invest ten thousand dollars with him the day he was in my office. I gave him almost all my savings. I don't make a lot of money in this job, but I do try to save what I can. I can't be club manager forever. Your father promised me my investment would double within three years. He said I needed to grow my money."

Anna recognized her father's spiel. Make your investment grow to shelter you like a giant oak in your retirement. Bull, bull, and more bull.

Once more her father left a victim for her to trip over. "Alan, I'm so sorry. I knew nothing about this."

He must have moved in on Alan the first day he came to the club.

Alan glanced out the window that looked out over the golf course and drew in a breath. "Contrary to widely held belief, I know you're telling me the truth. I wasn't lying when I said it was a pleasure working with you. You're a good young woman, and I'm really sorry I can't keep you here."

"So, you believe me?"

"Yes. I pride myself on picking out talented people to employ, and I can't believe there's a possibility I misjudged you. No, you were never a part of your father's schemes. Your worst crime was lying about your past to keep yourself from being associated with him."

"Thank you." She appreciated his kind words more than he would ever understand. It also meant wherever she went to next, he would give her a good recommendation. His belief in her took a lot of fear out of her future.

"Yes, well, there's still no way I can let you keep working here. I may trust you, but the clientele in this club will always wag their tongues about your father's crimes. You're poison to our membership. I hope you can understand my position." He opened the country club checkbook and began to write.

"Of course."

After scribbling out her name and the amount, he handed her the paycheck. "I was going to be set when that investment came in. I'm not sure what I'll do now."

"I don't know, but I can give you some insight about my father to help the police find him."

"I'm surprised they haven't questioned you."

"I've been sick. There's a chance Jenny was fielding all the calls coming into the house. After what he did to you, I'll do everything I can to make it right."

"I'd appreciate any help I can get." Alan closed the checkbook and sat behind his desk. He looked smaller sitting there. The padded shoulders of his suit jacket were slightly askew, and it looked as if he'd lost weight since she first met him.

Anna pulled out her phone and dialed her mother. "Hey, Mom. I'll be on the road soon. I was wondering. Do you know where Dad is?"

Anna listened to her mother chatter as she finally got around to a location. Even if they were divorced, they always checked in with each other. It was weird, but something her crazy parents did. "Thanks, Mom." She clicked off the phone. "He went to Chicago."

"I'll tell the police." Alan picked up his office phone.

"Hope you find him. Tell them he likes the Waldorf Astoria in Chicago."

"Isn't the Waldorf in New York?"

"Yes, but there's another one in Chicago. I'd try there first." Anna left the office. If her dad were in Chicago, she would go in the opposite direction, possibly as far as California. She needed to get as far away in order to be alone and free of him. As Anna passed the kitchen, she heard Caleb's voice, a little hoarse, but sounding like he was recovering from their shared cold. She would miss that little thrill that ran through her when he was close. It was exciting thinking he might step in any moment and brighten her day. Even though he never believed she was innocent and grouped her in with people she no longer cared for, in a crazy way, she was always happy to see him. Anna wasn't sure if she ever wanted to feel that way again with anyone, mostly because it hurt so much to lose it.

Anna trudged out to her car. She still needed to take a trip to the bank and cash her check before she left. Cyrus Armstrong got out of a Jeep Wrangler and called to her. So far, he'd been a man of few words, but today he closed the distance between them.

"There you are. I heard you were sick. How are you feeling?"

"Better. Thanks, Mr. Armstrong."

"I'm glad. Caleb just got back to work himself. I was on my way in to check on him. Silly, I know. He's a grown man, but he's been having a rough time lately. I guess I need to check on you, too."

"Thank you, but I'm not back at work. I got fired."

Cyrus nodded, a wise look in his eyes. "I figured that might happen. It's their loss. What will you do now? We've only recently been getting to know the new you. I guess it's our loss, too."

The kindness of Cyrus's words hit Anna hard. After holding it together since leaving the house, a rush of tears hit her. "I don't really know."

Cyrus thrust his hands in his pockets. "There, there. It can't be so very bad. The world is your oyster. You're young and beautiful and can throw a heck of a party. There are more event planner jobs out there. Whoever hires you gets a treasure. You did a topnotch job with the tournament. Heck, after hanging around with all those hobnobbers, I'm wondering if I should take up golf."

Cyrus's praise was endearing. It was fatherly, something she hadn't experienced in her life, and it filled a need she didn't realize she had. He looked so like Caleb. The same square jaw and soft eyes. Was this what Caleb would look like when he was older? Was Cyrus the kind of father he would be to their children? She stopped herself there. There would be no children. There would be no growing old with Caleb.

"You're right. I'll get another job, probably, but not here."

Cyrus pressed his lips together. "You wait and see. I firmly believe in every terrible day, there's a little good part you might have overlooked. Look for the good, Anna."

"Funny, that's exactly what I wanted people to do for me. Look for the good part of me, not the bad part they thought I was. Your son chose not to see past the bad."

"My son can be stubborn, and, as the Armstrong family representative, I'd like to apologize for his big mouth at the Cardinal Cafe. Even though he saved the Carmichaels from a bad investment, you can bet he got an earful from me. I only hope someday you can forgive him. He's as mixed up as you are. The two of you are so alike it hurts to watch you."

Anna scratched the side of her head. "We are?"

"Oh yeah. Only promise me you won't give up. When are you leaving town?"

"This afternoon. I'm getting the oil changed in my car and then I'm off."

"Okay. I hope you find your rainbow's end, sweetheart."

"Me too."

He reached out and clumsily patted her on the shoulder. It was sweet, if not a little awkward. As Cyrus walked away, there was one more thing she needed to do to make it right.

Chapter 37

Caleb was alerted by the sound of a car in the driveway of his parents' home as his mother sat on the front porch shelling beans. Anna got out of a car with an Uber sticker in the window. Something he couldn't understand stopped him from greeting her. He wanted to see how she talked to his mother when he wasn't there. If he ever had any doubt she was trying to live without conning people, this could confirm it. He positioned himself behind the curtain where he would have a clear view of the front porch.

Anna said something to the driver as she stepped out of the car. Caleb fought the instinct to go out and say something to her, but something held him back. He stayed next to the window, out of sight of Anna.

"Here you are again. Where's your car?" Beth asked.

"When I went to get my oil changed, I decided to sell it. It was a junker, anyway."

Beth looked suspicious. "If you say so." She waved at the driver. "Hey, Hal. Glad to see Anna is using your service. I told you someone would book you on the little appy thing."

"Making a little extra for my retirement. I drove a truck for thirty years. Simple to drive around people," Hal yelled through the open window.

"I should've realized you would know my Uber driver," Anna joked. "Only in Redbird Creek. I wanted to thank you for believing in me."

"No need to thank me. I've enjoyed getting to be around you again, and frankly, you're a lot nicer now than you were when you ran with those girls in high school. I never understood what Caleb saw in those girls. Now, don't you worry about anything. You're embarking on a new adventure, and I'll admit I'm a little jealous. You're going to be fine."

"When you put it that way, I guess you're right. I couldn't leave without making sure you got back the money my father stole from you."

Beth set the bowl down. "You don't have to pay me."

"Yes, I do." Anna handed her ten fresh one hundred-dollar bills. "I could never start over knowing I left behind something I should have fixed."

"If you're going around paying back all your daddy's victims, your final check from the country club isn't going to last very long."

"I know, and, as much as I'd like to, even I, the optimist, realize I can't. Seeing you has put a face to all the people who have trusted my father in the past. Thank you for that."

"Well, I guess I have my money back and will sock it into the bank before I do something else stupid with it. Safe travels, sweet girl."

Anna reached over and kissed Beth on the cheek. "Thanks for everything."

As Hal pulled away with Anna in the back seat, Caleb came out of the front door.

Beth held up the thousand dollars. "That sweet girl found a way to pay me back the thousand dollars I invested. It looks like she sold her car to get the money."

"About time." He crossed his arms as he watched Hal turn onto the road.

"Wasn't there anything you wanted to say to Anna?" Beth asked quietly.

"Goodbye? Don't steal from my family again?"

Beth stood up, straightened her apron, and deposited the money in her pocket. She raised a hand and pointed a finger at Caleb, as if he were a small boy. "Caleb Armstrong. It's time we settled this thing between you two."

"What?"

Beth's eyes widened. "You think you can hide it, but you're in love with Anna. Yet, there you hid behind the screen door, too afraid to come out. That isn't the man I raised. You can do better."

"I wasn't hiding. I was simply passing through a room. And, for your information, I'm not in love with her."

"Bull." Beth slapped her knee. "You're so smitten it hurts me to watch. You need to stop her and stop her now. A love like this only comes along once in a man's life, and you're about to miss it because of your stubbornness. Are you willing to live with the regret of letting the woman you love leave? You need to fight for this. Don't wait, Caleb."

Caleb started to speak but stopped. Anna was leaving and this was the second he had the chance to stop her. It was up to him. He reached into his pocket and produced his keys. "This is crazy. You better be right."

"I'm your mother." Beth smiled. "I'm always right."

Caleb hopped into his pickup parked around the side of the house and sped off down the driveway. The Uber had pulled onto the main road and was speeding along nicely. Caleb sat on the horn, trying to get Hal to pull over. The lights on the car flashed, giving him the signal to pass.

He flashed his lights back and waved.

He saw her tap Hal on the shoulder. The car slowed, and Hal pulled over and parked on the shoulder.

Anna scrambled out of the car, and yelled, "What is wrong with you?"

Caleb bounded out of the truck and ran across the gravel on the side of the road, his feet pounding with every step. He reached out and pulled Anna in. The gray clouds gave out a low rumble of thunder as Caleb kissed her. The rain began to pour down in sheets and, as their lips touched, their faces and hair became drenched. They laughed and kissed more as she slid her arms around his neck, oblivious to the weather. He groaned and his hand caressed her back as the rain continued around them. Finally, they pulled away.

"Was that goodbye?" Anna yelled through the pounding rain. "A simple handshake would have been fine."

"Not goodbye. Hello." He kissed her again, and again. Finally, he lifted his head and whispered into her hair. "Don't go."

"I have to. There's nothing left for me here."

"I'm here."

Anna drew in a breath. "You are? Do you mean you want me to stay, even though I'm–"

"I love you, Anna. I love your stubbornness, your ability to make me laugh, and mostly the way you make me feel like I can't wait for every day to roll by hoping for the chance I'll get to be with you again."

"But what about my father?"

"What about him? You're not your father. I was so wrong. You're an honest woman with the poor fortune of being born to a father who is a criminal. Don't worry. I'm sure Al Capone's daughter went through the same thing."

Anna laughed and pushed at Caleb's shoulder.

"Get out of the rain and go inside, you crazy lovebirds." Caleb's brother Sam was driving by and yelled out the window while he honked the horn. "And it's about time."

Caleb tightened his grip on her waist. His heart was hammering against hers. "For once, I agree with my brother. I would so like to go someplace quiet and dry off with you. Will you stay?" Caleb looked into the eyes gently holding his soul. He wasn't Park Avenue, and he never would be. Would it be enough for her?

"There's nowhere else I'd rather be. No other person I'd rather be with. I'm still trying to figure out how it happened, but I love you too, Caleb Armstrong."

They kissed again while more cars drove by honking horns and cheering.

Anna pulled away. "I've come home to a place I never want to leave again. For the first time in my life I'm looking forward to the future, and you, Caleb Armstrong, are a big part of it."

"And you," he whispered tenderly, his love for her nearly bursting out of him, "are definitely a part of mine. Who knew a girl with a broken shoe would wobble right into my heart."

"Stop." She playfully shook him, her arms still circling his waist.

"Never. I love you, Anna."

"Back at you."

Epilogue

Six months later.

"Put the flowers over there, Gladys."

Gladys toted a crystal vase full of white roses, clumping across the floor in her heels. Gladys was not used to wearing a heel anywhere above an inch. Her walk resembled something between a hurt bear and a fullback.

"Yes, Anna. As your maid of honor," she gave a little nod with her chin, "I will move them wherever you wish for them to be, oh honorable bride. Are you sure you should still be here? You need to get dressed. Why are you waiting? If I were getting married, I'd sleep in my wedding dress the night before."

"Trust me, after opening my own event planning business, I'm quite able to juggle more than one thing at a time."

"Yes, you've proven how talented you are in multi-tasking, but not today. Go get dressed. I can handle whatever needs doing around here." Gladys stepped to a mirror and plumped her carefully set, curled brown hair. She looked beautiful, in a Gladys kind of way.

"Is your allergist guy on his way?"

Gladys beamed. "He sure is," she stated in her newly clear, congestion-free voice. Her new boyfriend, Norm, not only wooed her, but cured her allergies. Her nose was no longer patchy red, and she possessed a surprisingly lovely voice.

"Anna, get back here," Beth motioned from the doorway. "We need to put the dress on you." She was happily overwhelmed as now she would have two mothers in her life.

"I'm coming." She made her way across the church fellowship hall.

When she rushed in, Beth steered her over to the makeshift dressing area. "I think I'm more nervous than you are. It doesn't help my son has been walking on pins and needles for weeks. The sooner you two get hitched, the better. I can't stand the drama anymore. He could star in one of those temperamental chef cooking shows, he's so uptight."

A niggling thought occurred to Anna as she pulled off her robe and stepped into the heap of white satin. "Maybe he's having second thoughts?"

Beth smiled and fastened the back of the dress. "Oh, honey, not at all. No, he's the kid who jumps on the bed at five on Christmas morning because he can't wait to open up all those boxes under the tree."

Anna's mother, Lillian, came in, wearing a lovely pastel purple dress. She smelled of Shalimar and fine-milled soap. "It's what family is all about. Having someone you love stretch you beyond patience. Trust me, I know."

Lillian brought her new litigation-happy lawyer with her to the wedding and although the guy was a little pushy, Anna liked him. He was a marked improvement over her own father. The police tracked down her father in Chicago, and he was now serving another five-year sentence for the same crime he'd been jailed for before. At least this time there weren't so many victims trying to put their lives back together. McKinzie's father saw to that by giving a lengthy testimony at the trial.

McKinzie was still single among her friends at the country club but had shifted her focus to the new tennis coach. Once again, she targeted the staff who served the rich instead of the rich themselves.

Jenny came running in with a cookie and threw her bag in the corner. "You should taste these. My brother is an artiste."

She held the cookie up for Anna to take a quick bite.

"Stop that," Beth chided. "If you get chocolate on this dress, you'll live to regret it."

"Sorry, Mom. Caleb has had his staff cooking all week at the event center. I only hope he hasn't worn himself out. It's amazing how you two have turned the old skating rink around." Jenny quickly started changing into the bridesmaid dress like a firefighter going to a four-alarm fire.

"One thing I've learned is cooking is meditation for him." Anna straightened the shoulders of her dress. The wedding gown was absolutely stunning but amazingly comfortable.

"I suppose so." Jenny gave a wistful smile. "I'm sure going to miss having you for a roommate. You are hands-down the best renter I've ever had. Definitely the most interesting."

Anna smiled at Jenny. "There was no way I ever would have made it through all this without you. Don't worry. You'll have a new boarder soon, I hope."

"Yeah, but it will sure be lonely."

Beth smiled. "Don't worry, Daughter. Someone will come along for you."

Anna wondered if she meant a new renter or her own true love. That was something she liked about Beth. It was important to listen because sometimes her simple words relayed a lot more than you thought.

There was a light tapping on the door. Alan stuck his head in.

"Are you ready?" He extended an arm.

"I guess so." Anna did one last check in the mirror in the makeshift changing room. Everything was in its place. Hair, gown hanging straight, makeup, veil. She took one step forward and wobbled on her heels. She purposely wobbled herself again, just to make sure. This was one day she wouldn't be breaking a heel.

As they stepped into the church, she was surprised to see so many people in attendance. Not only were all the members of the country club there, but everyone who worked there as well.

Caleb stood at the front with his brother Sam, fidgeting. When his gaze lit on Anna, a calm came over him and he stopped and stood still, and Anna grinned, her heart filling with warmth. Yeah, this was right.

Anna held tight to Alan's arm, feeling like she was finally where she needed to be. When Caleb took her hand, a rush came over her. She glanced back over the gathered crowd, her gaze lighting on the Armstrongs and Gladys. These were the people of Redbird Creek and she was proud to be one of them.

As Alan quietly left Anna to stand facing Caleb, she sighed.

"Are you ready for this?" Caleb whispered.

"I can't wait," Anna whispered back.

"Then let's get cooking, Anna." They turned to face the minister and begin their new life together.

Don't miss out!

Visit the website below and you can sign up to receive emails whenever Teresa Trent publishes a new book. There's no charge and no obligation.

https://books2read.com/r/B-A-FJQD-FVEUB

BOOKS 2 READ

Connecting independent readers to independent writers.

Also by Teresa Trent

Pecan Bayou
A Dash of Murder
Overdue for Murder
Doggone Dead
Buzzkill
Burnout
Murder for a Rainy Day
Till Dirt Do Us Part
Oh Holy Fright
Die a Yellow Ribbon

Piney Woods
Murder of a Good Man

Redbird Creek
The Con Man's Daughter

Watch for more at https://teresatrent.com.

About the Author

Teresa Trent writes the Pecan Bayou and Piney Woods Mystery Series, both of which take place in Texas. Pecan Bayou is in the Hill Country of Texas and Piney Woods is in East Texas. Same state, two completely different places. Teresa lives in Houston Texas with her family and has been writing mysteries for over a decade. You can visit her website at TeresaTrent.com.

Read more at https://teresatrent.com.